PERSONAL WAR

PART 2

DAVE AQUINO

CCB Publishing
British Columbia, Canada

Personal War Part 2

ISBN-13 978-0-9809191-1-0
First Edition

Library and Archives Canada Cataloguing in Publication

Aquino, Dave, 1981-
Personal War Part 2 / written by Dave Aquino.
ISBN 978-0-9809191-1-0
I. Title.
PS3601.Q557P47 2008 813'.6 C2008-900163-X

Publisher: CCB Publishing
British Columbia, Canada
www.ccbpublishing.com

Contents

Chapter 1

The Newspaper

A city newspaper had been thrown on the cherry wood coffee table. As William Defreno wandered around his Reseda condo, he appreciated anew his better life. Unlike his rotten old house sitting a thousand miles away, his new condo was not rented.

A glance around the clean modern home showed it fitted with all stainless steel appliances in the kitchen, matching cherry wood furniture in the living area and a king-sized bed in one of the two bedrooms. Even though the artwork on the wall was inexpensive, with proper lighting and framing it passed as trendy. The wall also contained a studio photograph of William and his girlfriend, Jennifer Annie Lewis. William took the picture off the wall and held it.

"Oh Annie, you're so great," William said to her smiling image. Although her first name was Jennifer, William liked calling her Annie instead. She didn't mind. Even though they weren't married William knew she would be the one he wanted to wed.

The only thing that upset the harmony of the place was that small town newspaper. After sitting on the brushed leather sofa he put the picture on the coffee table and grabbed the phone to make a long distance call. With the paper in one hand and now the receiver against his shoulder, he grabbed his morning coffee.

"District Attorney Janet Cellers's office, may I help you?"

The other end answered.

"Yes," William said as he set down the coffee and moved the paper to that hand. "I'm calling from the *State Evening Post*. I'm interested in this story about the Casner family."

"Oh, hold on. I'll let Janet herself talk to you."

"Great!" After ten minutes on hold listening to reject Jazz music and sipping coffee she came on.

"This is Janet."

"Yes, I wanted to get a story from you about the news of the Casner family."

"Well, that's a bad one."

"I saw that in the paper. How bad is it?"

"Pretty much the officer arrested, that would be Officer Marshall, was murdered along with a school counselor a few months ago."

"Yeah, I heard."

"Well, Marshall was going to testify against Randy and Carol Casner in exchange for a lesser sentence. Now, the office is having a hell of time prosecuting the Casner case."

"Go on."

"Well, no money was found at the Casner home and the Casners claim the house itself was bought with Mr. Casner's inheritance.

"I've followed this story before. If I remember right, traces of meth were found in the home."

"Yes, but no traces that it was being manufactured there. Officer Marshall was the key and we can't prove Marshall and the Casners were working together."

"But they were, weren't they?"

"I believe so, but no witnesses ever came forward and our anonymous tipster can't be found."

"Oh, well, the Casners are gonna get something, aren't

they?"

"Can we go off the record for a minute," Janet whispered.

"Sure," William replied as his heartbeat kicked up a notch.

"Okay, once again off the record, the only thing the Casners are gonna get is their home back and their cars back. The Casner lawyer, Mr. Miller, is amazing. Because of the fact that we can't prove drug trafficking and selling charges, Miller wants even the small charges of possession and IRS fraud dropped as compensation for falsely arresting them."

"What? So the Casners are gonna walk completely and get an apology from the DA's office? What else does Casner want? A dozen roses as well?"

"I know. This man paid off law enforcement and made almost a million dollars off drugs and is gonna get away with it."

"Oh, and not to mention that he was the reason William Defreno killed himself."

"Ya know, I often wonder if that Defreno kid was set up by the Casners. Marshall's testimony is what convicted that kid and if he was working for Casner as well…"

"Yeah."

"Well, we are still off the record, right?"

"Yes."

"I not supposed to say this, but why not?"

"What is it, Miss Cellers?"

"Whoever the anonymous tipster was probably saw Casner and Marshall together."

"Probably," William stuttered.

"If we could find this person and they would testify at the pre trial, that would be enough to scare the Casners into a deal."

"What kinda deal?"

"Right now all they will accept is a full dismissal of the charges. I want to offer him a deal; no more than eight years."

"Gee, that sounds familiar."

"Why is that?"

"Oh," William stuttered as he forgot for a second that she didn't know she was talking to the kid she put away for fourteen years; or so she thought.

"Anyway," Cellers said. "I need that tipster by the next two weeks or I have no choice but to dismiss all charges."

"I see."

"Listen, the First Amendment says freedom of the press."

"Yeah, so?"

"Technically I can't ask you to publish that the anonymous tipster needs to come forward, but you could do it anyway and since I maintain it's off the record I'm covered."

"I catch your drift."

"Please, sir," Cellers begged. "I need to find this person in two weeks."

"Miss Cellers, I'm a writer, so in my years of experience I would say that the anonymous man might incriminate himself if he came forward."

"Good point. However, once again off the recor--" she stuttered. "Oh, the hell with it, put it in the paper that I will offer full immunity if they will testify in two weeks. Please tell them to call me. Heck they can call me collect if they please."

"Okay, will do."

"Please, I gotta have 'em within two weeks or the Casners are free to go."

"Thank you for your time, ma'am," William hung up.

Without delay he left the condo and got into his restored '65 Lincoln. The palm trees swaying on each side of the highway had to mean it was windy, but William was not thinking about weather. After a few miles he arrived at the Vons Supermarket where Annie worked.

"Hey, babe," William said.

Annie smiled and walked toward him. Her shoulder length blond hair and pretty smile gave William a heavenly feeling. With a little bit of extra weight on her and unpainted nails she looked feminine, but healthy and self-assured as well. Once again his past came to mind and reminded him how lucky he was to have her and to no longer be on the brink of poverty.

"Hey, I get off work in twenty minutes."

"Okay, I'll wait."

"Nah, I think I'll just have someone cover for me."

"You sure?"

"It's the American way, honey."

With arms around each other they left the store and went to a nearby sushi bar. After a plate of many different raw fish and other sea creatures was brought to them, William finally told her the news.

"Oh God," Annie said.

"I know. If I don't go back and testify against the Casners, they will both walk free."

"I don't know, honey," Annie said, trying to use chopsticks to eat her rice. After seeing William didn't even bother to try his sticks she used her spoon.

"I can't let Casner walk, this man was my demise."

"He is the reason we are together."

"No, I am the reason and you are the reason. Casner was the reason we almost didn't get to meet."

Annie agreed and saw the sadness in William's eyes.

"William, we're in California, this Casner is a thousand miles away from you. He can't harm us."

"Yeah, I thought about that. Also if I go back everyone will know I'm not dead."

"Plus, won't you have to serve fourteen years for what you got convicted of?"

"Actually Cellers said she'd offer immunity."

"I don't know. It's so scary for you to go back, what if something goes wrong?"

"Yes, I didn't bring this up because I wanted to argue with you. The truth is I don't know if I even want to go back. That's what I like about you. I feel I can have a legitimate conversation and we can both agree. Really, should I care? Or should I say let 'em get away with it as long as I'm not affected?"

"Well," Annie said, grimacing slightly at the taste of the octopus she had just eaten. "Let's do a pros and cons."

"Okay, we already know the cons. Some pros would be that I could be me again. I wouldn't have to hide behind the name Pat Bateman. I could visit mom instead of having to have secret letters sent to her. I mean, how long am I gonna be okay with the fact that I don't exist and I'm technically a wanted fugitive?

"If I ever get arrested or printed they'll know I'm William Defreno and this might be the only chance I get to receive immunity. Finally, I could let the Casners know I'm here. They think I'm dead and that they won. It would be so nice to have my charges lifted and actually be able to see Mitch and Riley again. To not have to pretend I'm dead."

"Also, to bring justice on the Casners. Anyone who would harm you is hated by me," Annie added.

"This is why I like you, Annie. Because instead of just fighting with me over it, you are willing to open up and do what is best for us."

"Why else do you like me, William?"

"Because when I make a mistake, instead of saying 'you should've done it' or 'what the hell's wrong with you?' you will help come up with a solution."

"Yeah, I know I hate it when people do that. It's like, I know I should've done it, but it's done; now what can we do?"

"You know, also I feel like we are on a team. It's not me versus you; we work together. We bought a condo together and it wasn't all just my money."

"I love to hear why you like me."

"Oh, a con would be that if Casner knew I was alive he might mess with us."

"Hell no! Listen, after we go and put him away we'll come home. I don't think you'll argue with that. Besides I'd like to see him try to mess with us from jail."

"Was I mistaken when I heard the word 'we'?

"No, I'll come with you. We'll do it this weekend after you get assurance from Cellers that all your charges will be dismissed."

"I will. Why do you wanna come?"

"You need me. Like you said, we are a team. Besides, I'd like to meet Mitch and Riley. Oh and your mom. Oh and this Melissa girl; I'd love to see the look on her face when she sees you've got a real girlfriend."

"I guess you can meet the Casners. I myself would love to see them in chains and orange jumpsuits. Last time when it was me in chains they laughed at me from the gallery."

The couple held hands and smiled. It was clear that this was no crush or sexual infatuation, but the real thing.

"Are you sure about this, Annie?"

"I'm with you; let's do it."

William smiled. "Your car or mine?"

"Yours. You said you drove the same car when you lived there."

"Well, kinda. It was rough. Hey, I'd love to introduce you to Redneck Roy."

"This will be great. I mean you met my mom and know all about me. But everything is top secret with you."

"I guess that's another pro. You can finally know what I went through out there. And once I'm cleared you can call me William in public. Wow, to think I'll never have to worry about the Casners or those charges ever coming back on me."

"It's worth it, William Defreno."

"Hey hey hey," William said, laughing. "I'm not cleared yet. William Defreno is wanted and now I'm really wanted, but in a good way. Well, I guess a better word for me now is needed not wanted."

"Well, wanted too. Casner isn't the only one who wants you."

"Oh really?" William said as he moved closer to her. After they finished the sushi they went to the restaurant patio and watched the sunset.

"Annie I just had a thought."

"What?"

"After we get back, let's get married."

"You serious?"

"Yeah, let's just do. It'll be great we can actually marry as William and Annie Defreno. I mean it, the whole thing. We'll go to Vegas, limos and a honeymoon in Hawaii."

"I can't wait. I thought you'd never ask."

"Well, I would've asked earlier but it's kinda embarrassing that I don't have a name. I mean, come on, imagine the minister saying 'do you mystery man take this woman.'"

"Yeah," Annie replied with a laugh.

Chapter 2

Back in Town

After the weekend driving across the country, the town was only two miles away.

"Hold on, pull over," William said to Annie, who had been driving the final hundred miles.

"What is it?"

"I just--well can't believe I'm back. I mean everyone thinks I'm dead, and in a way when I left here I was."

"Come on. It'll be good to face this again."

As they pulled up to the courthouse William could visualize himself coming out of that very building a guilty man. The thought that one day he'd be coming back to clear himself seemed too unreal. After his plan came off he figured that was it; he would never be cleared. Few people were around; nobody recognized him yet.

When they arrived they met with Janet Cellers. She was astonished to see him since she had thought him dead. He was uneasy as well since the last time he saw her was when she convicted him.

"Wow, Mr. Defreno, it really is you."

"Yes, and this is my girlfriend, Annie."

"Well, I just need your signature on my immunity agreement."

"This covers everything?"

"Yep, all charges you were convicted of, any charges that could relate to your testimony against Mr. Casner and any civil charges. As long as you testify today against the Casners you will be completely clean."

"Not a problem," William said as he signed the agreement.

"Okay, William, in about an hour you'll be called out. I hope the Casners accept my offer once they see you're a witness."

"Don't worry, I'll be quite convincing," William said as he hugged Annie and smiled.

"One last thing, William. You get immunity no matter what. I just gotta know. I just always wondered, did you throw yourself in front of his car?"

"No, he hit me because I broke his track record. The charges you convicted me of were false."

"Okay," Cellers said with a bit of relief.

In the courtroom Mr. and Mrs. Casner and Casner's lawyer Mr. Miller were well dressed and looking confident. Although they were in deep trouble they talked about how good things were. None of them noticed William and Annie enter the courtroom nor that their conversation was no longer private from the lights and judging eyes of Annie and William.

"Yes," Carol Casner said. "Once we get outta here we're still taking the cruise line."

"Good," Miller replied. "How's Julie doing?"

"Oh, wonderful as always, she's spending the summer in Italy for her internship."

"Wow, she grew up so fast. It seems like just yesterday she was a little bundle of joy."

"Well, I'm so proud of her and I hope she meets a good-looking Italian man while she is there."

"Oh she will. I'm sure guys are lined up out the door to marry her."

"Oh yes indeed."

"Good, you been hanging in there? I know this stupid thing has to be stressful."

"Oh, of course. Besides I never doubted we'd win, we never lose anything."

"Neither do I. Once we get this crap cleared I wanna sue the city for the false arrest. Too bad I can't order they dig up William Defreno and put him in the electric chair for stalking you."

"Oh yes, how tragic that Marshall was killed."

"Oh I know," Randy Casner interrupted. "The two of us were talking when he got the call he died on."

"Well I'm sure there are more good cops like Marshall," Miller said with a grin.

William grinned as well. Seeing them so cocky and confident that they were going to get away with their crimes removed any regret about coming. Annie nodded her head and realized William had never exaggerated the maliciousness of the Casners.

"Your honor," Cellers started. "I intend to prove that we have enough evidence to go to trial here. I intend to prove that the Casners were selling and manufacturing methamphetamine. I also intend to prove that the late Officer Marshall worked for the Casners to help them avoid arrest and corner the market with law enforcement interference."

"Your honor," Mr. Miller interrupted. "I ask the court that all charges be dropped today. It is clear that all the evidence the state has is circumstantial. There is no trace of any money that can't be accounted for, no witnesses, and Officer Marshall was murdered."

"Miss Cellers," Judge Foster said. "Mr. Miller is right. You have very little evidence and unless you have something more I have no choice but to dismiss all charges today."

"I know," Cellers replied with a smile. "I have a witness you will find very informing."

"Well call him up, 'cause right now you have nothing."

"Your honor, Mr. Miller, members of the court, I would like to call William Defreno to the stand."

"What?" Miller blurted, followed by a laugh. Mr. and Mrs. Casner laughed as well. The laugher silenced instantly as William walked up to the stand. Annie smiled at William and he back at her.

"Is this a joke?" Miller asked.

"Nope," Cellers replied.

"William Defreno is dead, burned beyond recognition."

"Your honor, could you tell Mr. Miller to stop interrupting me."

"Mr. Miller, please don't speak unless spoken to."

"Mr. Defreno," Cellers started after William was sworn in. "Can you tell me what you observed the day of your sentencing?"

"Yes, I went to the Casner house and hid in the bushes. I had stolen a dead body from the morgue my buddy worked at. I was gonna burn the body in my car with some gasoline to fake my death. I wanted to do it in front of their house. I wanted them to know they were responsible for it. Before I completed my task I saw Marshall, Mrs. Casner and Timothy Hamlin outside the house."

"What were they doing?"

"Talking. I was close enough to hear what was said. Not only that, close enough to see the briefcase in Mrs. Casner's hand."

"What were they talking about?"

"The price of meth. Marshall stated that meth costs about eight grand a pound and that he was getting it for about two grand and that he had twenty pounds. Mrs. Casner stated that she couldn't believe she was holding a hundred grand in that briefcase."

"Then what?"

"Then I lit the gas rag and ran. I never looked back; I just heard the explosion. The three of them heard it too."

"What did they do?"

"They examined the car and my supposed dead body. One even joked that they didn't have to go to my sentencing now. Then they solved the only imperfection of my faked death."

"What flaw was that?"

"Well, any dental record check could've proven the body in the car was not me. But Marshall insisted that he didn't want ATF or FBI agents around the Casner house."

"Why not?"

"Because they might smell the 'merchandise' as he put it in the basement of the Casner home. So Marshall said he would have the car and body destroyed and tell the papers I drove off a cliff."

"Your honor, I'd like to enter this backdated newspaper into evidence."

"What's the relevance?"

"In the newspaper it did say that William Defreno drove off a cliff so it backs his testimony today."

"Evidence entered."

"No further questions, your honor."

Next it was Mr. Miller's turn to cross examine the witness. William cringed at the fact that this was the same lawyer who helped Randy Casner get the civil charges dismissed after he ran over William. This time instead of the cocky 'I'm gonna railroad you' swagger, Miller seemed slightly panicked.

"So, Mr. Defreno, you're just back from the dead huh?"

"I was never dead. Besides you're the one who just said you wished I was alive so you could ask the court to put me in the electric chair for stalking your clients."

"Your honor, I want it noted for the record that he admitted he was stalking my clients."

"Does that mean the statements he just referred to were true?"

"I'm not at liberty to answer that."

"Fine, noted."

"Yep, stalking, William, is a felony. That's what you are, a felon. Anything you say should be dismissed as ridiculous!" Miller shouted.

"Mr. Miller, tone it down or you're outta here."

"Yes, your honor. Anyway, why did you kill yourself or want everyone to think you were dead?"

"Because I was going to be sentenced that day up to fourteen years."

"But now you have been offered some sort of deal in exchange for your lying testimony today."

"Objection," Cellers yelled.

"Sustained. You better watch it counsel."

"Actually, I got full immunity."

"Oh, you walk as long as you come here? It all makes sense. You broke the law and like always want to blame my clients and get away with it. Now that your fake death didn't work you want to try something new, right?"

"I didn't need immunity. I was considered dead and nobody bothered to look for me. In fact I didn't get caught. I could've lived forever never having to spend a day in jail. I really don't have much to gain for coming here today. In fact it is risky to come here and do this."

"Well, your honor, I can prove William is imprecise in his testimony. You said that Mrs. Casner said she had a hundred grand in the suitcase. Then, that Marshall said four grand per pound and that he had twenty pounds. Is that your testimony?"

"Yes."

"Well that only adds up to eighty grand. Why would she bring a hundred? You just made that up and didn't think it through."

"Thank you for reminding me. The other twenty grand was a bribe to Marshall for falsely arresting me and perjuring himself in court to get me convicted."

Miller and the Casners looked at each other in grief; all three wished they had communicated better and that Miller had not asked that question.

"What were you charged with Mr. Defreno?"

"Conspiracy to commit murder in the first degree, resisting arrest and two counts of habitual harassment."

"So you want us to believe someone who conspired to commit murder?"

"Objection," Cellers yelled.

"Overruled. Mr. Defreno was convicted of those charges."

"Well, like I said Marshall was paid twenty grand to falsely arrest me because I broke a track record and--"

"Mr. Defreno, why did--"

"No, don't interrupt me," William said louder. "This is my day! This man drove me to want to die. Used drug money to pay off the law. Used drug money to try to put me away for a crime I didn't commit. When they did see me dead in front of their house they didn't even care. In fact they laughed about it. That's why I came here, for justice on them."

"Mr. Defreno that's all--"

"I'm not done! They even hired someone who looked like me to rob a bank so it would look like I did it. I'll never claim that I'm completely innocent, but they not only started this war but continued with it long after I wanted to call it quits. I mean I surrendered basically. They win I lose, but it wasn't enough. They still had to kick me when I was down."

"Okay, Mr. Defreno," Foster said, "I am going to have to ask you to stop."

"Yes, of course."

"Well, your honor, I hope you see what a delusional lunatic this witness is."

"Mr. Miller, I'm the judge. I'll decide who's crazy and who's not."

"Now, Mr. Defreno, I take it you were the one who stole the hundred grand?"

"No, I ran as far away from there as possible after I heard the explosion."

"So who did steal the money? You were the only one there. I want this man arrested for theft because the Casners never found it."

A slight panic hit William because his immunity didn't cover the theft since he never told Cellers that he took the money. As she stood up William just hoped she wasn't going to ask the bailiff to cuff him.

"Whoa!" Cellers yelled. "Your honor, I want it noted it was admitted that this hundred grand in a briefcase did exist. They just admitted that what Mr. Defreno said was true."

William could see the look of "oh crap" in Miller's and in the Casner's eyes.

"No more questions," Miller said wanted to slink away from this mess.

"Mr. Defreno, you may step down." William stepped down and sat next to Annie who held hands with him.

"After hearing the testimony today I see probable cause to go to trial with this case. Adjourned."

William and Annie left the courtroom and went to the courthouse cafe. After their coffee they were just about to leave the courthouse when Janet Cellers stopped them.

"You did wonderfully William."

"I hope the jury thinks so. Anyway, when is the trial so I can plan to come back?"

"You don't need to come back, you're free to leave."

"You don't need me again?"

"Nope. The Casners and their lawyer agreed on a plea bargain."

"The bargain of no more than eight years?"

"Oh no, not that one. That was before we knew about the hired bank robbery and a confession of having a hundred grand. The new bargain is a minimum of ten years, but no more than fifteen."

"Oh God, we did it!"

"Yes, but what did happen to that hundred grand?" Cellers asked with an allegation of guilt towards William in her tone.

"Probably a kid found it. He'll get to drink all the Big Gulps he wants now."

"Yeah, probably, anyway thank you William," Cellers said as she put out her hand for William to shake. As he did he just couldn't believe he would ever have shaken hands with her.

Chapter 3

Wedding Bells

"You two getting married someday?"

"Yes, as soon as we get home."

"Well, I don't eat much, so if you want to invite me I'd love to come."

As he Annie went outside a flashback of his conviction day came to mind; the thought of how dark and dreary the outside looked at the time. The hopelessness he felt as the Casners smiled at his demise.

Now it felt like everything was back in color. The sun shone and flowers of many colors bloomed. William looked at Annie and saw beautiful cumulus clouds mirrored in her blue eyes. This was heaven for him.

Before leaving they decided to visit Mitch and Riley.

"I just have two words to say," William stated. "It's alive."

"Oh my God, it is you," Riley said.

"You're back," Mitch added.

"Well, only for a little bit. Were going home tomorrow. This is my soon to be wife, Annie."

"Hello," Mitch and Riley said. William explained how he had cleared himself and put the Casners away.

"So what else did I miss while I was away?" William asked.

"Well, Joe is on the Rose City police reserve."

"Where the hell is that?"

"Some bubble-fuck town in the middle of Kansas. I mean he's just on their reserve in case the eight cops in the town get overloaded."

"Wow, and they say dreams can't come true."

"Let's see, Marshall and the middle school counselor were murdered and the case is unsolved. A. R. oh, I mean Frank, works as a secretary in an office."

"Oh my, a secretary?"

"Yeah," Mitch added. "I hope the office manager doesn't sexually harass him."

"So, how 'bout you, William? When's the wedding?"

"Probably a month or two."

"Well, now that it's not illegal for us to be together can we come to the wedding?"

"Yep. Well, better be careful or Marshall might arrest you and anyone else who is at my wedding," William said sarcastically.

"Yeah, Annie might get put in jail as well for contacting you. Remember nobody is to have contact with you except family," Mitch said referring to a warning Officer Marshall had once given them. William smiled again at the fact that he could finally laugh at Marshall's warning for everyone to stay away from him.

"Well, guys, me and Annie are gonna get something to eat."

"Let me guess," Riley said. "Moe's Diner?"

"Yes, Moe's Diner."

"Well, have a good one."

"Don't worry. This time I won't be leaving for so long. You'll see me again at my wedding."

"Cool. You wanna invite Frank?"

"Maybe he could guard the place in case the communists invade the chapel."

"I told you he's a secretary, maybe he could do your paperwork."

"Anyway, I'll stop by before we leave tomorrow and you guys try to get some time off for the wedding."

"You got it, dude," Mitch replied. As they left, Mitch seemed a bit melancholy. He was happy to have William back but it wasn't the same. Now that he had Annie he wouldn't want to do the crazy things they did while they were in school. Mitch also realized that William was the first one of his circle of friends to get married. He knew Riley would be next and he and Frank would probably never marry.

After leaving his friends William and Annie took a tour of the city in the Lincoln.

"There's my old high school."

"Where you got expelled?"

"Yeah, and I'll show you the junkyard and Redneck Roy."

After showing her all the sights, Redneck Roy, his mother, and explaining their significance it was off to Moe's Diner."

"You know, William, this city is creepy and everyone like, I don't know, had their noses stuck up in the air for no reason."

"It's a rich town. I was the only who was poor here."

"Yeah right. I bet everyone here could live a hundred years and still not pay off the amount of debt they're in. They're up to their ears."

At Moe's Diner Lois was working all by herself. The place seemed bigger but still not fancy enough to be a fine restaurant.

"William, I wondered when you were gonna come and want your job back."

"Actually I came to eat here with my girlfriend."

"Does she want a job here?"

"Afraid not. We're going home tomorrow."

"Well, I now have hotel rooms at this place. Want one for the night?"

"Free?"

"Of course not, but at thirty bucks a night it pretty much is free."

"Same ole Lois," William said softly to Annie.

"Yeah, a lot has changed. I expanded the menu and the hotel rooms bring in some good money."

"Can we stay at your mom's?" Annie asked.

"Yeah, but she'll probably bug the room we're in."

"Really?"

"No, but then she'll be spying on us all night."

"Okay let's stay here."

"I guess I'll try one out for the night."

"Good. Now what do you want to eat?"

"Two steak and shrimps well done and two glasses of the expensive house red wine. Oh and don't use the fancy bottle that's been refilled with cheap wine."

"I wouldn't do that."

"Yeah right."

"You are growing up. I remember when you couldn't even serve drinks, now you can drink them. You want coffee?"

"Yes."

"Regular or decaffeinated?"

"You forget that I know you just pour the regular in the decaffeinated pot to save money. So it doesn't really matter does it?"

"Oh yeah, you know all my corner cutting. You didn't tell your girlfriend about how I wash the plastic silverware and reuse it?"

"No, but thanks for reminding me."

"It seems like you were just a little kid when you worked here."

"Time flies, huh?"

"Are you two getting married?"

"Yes. I'll send you an invitation."

"Why not have it here? I'll cut you a great deal."

"Nope, Vegas all the way."

"Oh, okay, let me get your food."

After a nice meal and tons of memories and stories of working had come up it was time to hit the hay.

As they headed to Lois's hotel rooms that were actually converted storage rooms they both felt it was a complete rip-off for thirty dollars. Annie and William didn't argue that they had to stay in a dump hotel but instead enjoyed the circumstances.

"Well Annie, Lois needs the money and when we get to Vegas I wanna get the penthouse."

"This isn't bad. Besides, you've slept here before, right?"

"In the dumpster."

"Well, see? This is an upgrade."

"You really are great. I mean most girls would just bitch the whole time that this was a dump but you actually can make the best of it."

"Yes I can."

The next morning they left for California. In the car outside the diner William sat in confusion before starting the engine. Annie didn't think much of it at first.

"Didn't we have a full tank'a gas yesterday?"

"I guess we drove around too much."

"I swear it was full. Besides, it's not like me to run the tank down this low."

"I don't know, you lived here, maybe that Homie kid you told me about stole it to do a drive-by."

"I guess. I mean it's gone gone gone. If we don't get to a station soon we're gonna hafta push it."

"Okay, I'll push, you steer," Annie said with a smile.

"Actually there's a station real close. I remember I was always glad a station was close 'cause I had to earn money here before I could fill up. I've been so low it coasted into the station and ran to work to earn money to fill it up afterward."

As he drove away gas stains where his car had been parked were obvious. He nodded his head as it occurred to him it had obviously been siphoned but he didn't want to alarm Annie. There was still that chance the forty-year-old gas tank had a hole in it. In addition he thought, *if this is the worst thing that happens here this time, I'm lucky.*

His old gas station was only a block away. Memories arose of all the times he bought and pumped gas there and the worries and troubles that went through his mind when he did. A quick laugh came to mind that he once had to debate whether or not to steal the gas because he needed it but couldn't afford it. Now, he found it fun to return to this place a blissful changed man.

"I'm gonna get some snacks, want anything?" Annie asked.

"How 'bout some Luckys for old time's sake." Annie went inside giggling about him wanting Luckys. The only thing to foul the mood was a young man staring at William in a junk car. A closer look would have shown the bags under his eyes and the many cigarette butts by the car. It seemed fair to surmise that this kid had been waiting here for many hours for William to drive up.

After the snacks and smokes were purchased Annie wanted to get home. Inside she laughed at herself that she felt safer in Los Angeles than here in suburban America. As she got into the car with William the young man in his junk car tried to start it. After a few tries it coughed to life and he drove in front of William's car. With a patron behind him buying gas it was clear this kid had them trapped.

"Hey, move man," William said. No response came from the driver. All they could see was another cigarette flicked out the window followed by a small smoke cloud.

"Kid," Annie said in a rude tone, "we need to leave. Please

move your car."

Still no response, just another smoke cloud. William shut off his engine and he and Annie exited their vehicle.

"If the bum wants some money I'll give it to him," William said.

"I think he knows you. What the hell is wrong with him?"

"I don't know. Let me go see."

"No, I'll call the cops."

"Save it!" the kid yelled followed by a smoker's cough. "Hello, William. You look pretty healthy for a dead guy."

William froze at the sight of this well known kid dressed in rags and driving a junk car. The memories of the pretty and smooth face on this kid were history. All the envy of this kid being so good-looking and himself being plain were asinine now that his face was covered in zits, and bags under his eyes and nicotine stains marred his features.

"Oh my God."

"What!" Annie said as she stopped heading toward the payphone.

"So," he coughed, "who's the girl? Your sister?"

"No, Timmy."

"That's Tim to you punk."

"This is Timmy?" Annie wondered aloud.

"Yes, honey. I guess our tour wouldn't be complete without meeting him."

"I thought you said he was so cute and pretty? He looks like a frog who's smoked too many cigarettes."

"So, is it your sister, huh?"

"No."

"Oh," Timmy said waving his arms like a mad drunk. "That's too freakin' bad, 'cause if she was I could screw her and tape it then send it to your nice sunny condo in LA."

"Did you siphon my gas?"

"I don't know. Maybe it got up and flew away."

"I'll take that as a yes."

"What do you think of my car? It's a 1980 Honda Accord, gray with power nothing. Let's see, it's got many options, like maybe I should haul it to the junkyard or smash it with a lug wrench. It ain't nothing compared to your car."

Timmy got out and moved toward the Lincoln, walking around it in circles, angrily admiring it. William and Annie stayed back. Annie still had her heart set on calling the cops but it seemed this obnoxious kid just wanted to bug them a bit then he would leave. Judging by his lousy car if they could get unblocked it would be impossible for Timmy to follow the powerful Lincoln.

"Timmy, ya know, realistically yer car is actually fifteen years newer than mine."

"Hey, Tim," Annie added, "be glad you have a car. William hardly had one when he lived here. He would've loved to have this car on the days he had to walk to school. I'll bet many people would love a car like yours, especially with gas being so high."

Annie hoped to just baby talk this angry kid until the car behind them left and she and William could sneak away. The sweet words seemed to have no impact as Timmy continued walking in circles around the Lincoln and nodding his head.

"Ya know, Tim, with gas so high me and William probably wish we had a car like yours."

"Why?" Timmy coughed then caught his breath. "Why would you want a piece of shit like this when you have a shiny Lincoln? Who cares about high gas? If you can afford a car like this, surely you can afford the gas. So it's got cruise control. Oh my, look, power windows, power locks, power steering. What else, oh wow this paint is beautiful. Wow what a dreamboat. Oh and what could be better than having a chick in the passenger side as well?"

"Did you siphon my gas, yes or no?" William demanded.

"I mean a car says a lot about the driver. Let's see, yours says big gas guzzling pig who likes to waste money and likes fine dining. What else, hmm, let's see, oh yeah it says I'm better than anyone."

"Did you siphon my gas, yes or no?"

"Now, what does mine say? Hmm, oh yeah, it says poor lowlife who has to drive a piece of shit that's older than he is. Boy I'd say the two cars say a lot. What do you think?"

"I think you stole my gas."

"Well sure. But hey," he yelled with tears starting, "like you said, William, I'll just think like you. Since you have all the money in the world and I'm broke it's okay for me to steal your stuff, right? Isn't that what you taught me?"

"You're broke?"

"Yeah, parents are headed to jail."

"Now you know how I felt when you rubbed my face in it that you were so rich and preppy and I was poverty stricken. I had to work at the junkyard in the sun for pennies while you came in and spent two hundred and fifty dollars on a glove box door for your Hummer."

"That was you William, I was high class. I was gonna get to Yale after high school, or maybe KC med school or CU med school, maybe even Miami school of acting. I had all the options in the world. I was gonna maybe be a plastic surgeon or an actor, a makeup artist working at a major motion picture studio. Now look, I'm just a bum like you."

"Ahem!" Annie interrupted. "We are not bums, we live a nice lifestyle."

"Yeah, I remember nice lifestyle, but you stole it, William. You took my future away from me. This isn't the way it's supposed to be. I mean, you're white trash. You should be poor. That's where you belong, but me I'm supposed to be rich. Yes, you should be working for me and I'll make huge money while you make table scraps. This is an abomination."

"Well, now it's your turn to suffer," William replied as he and Annie were going to get in the car since the guy blocking them in from behind just left. Timmy quickly grabbed the keys out of the ignition of the Lincoln and walked away. William and Annie followed.

"We're not done talking yet. I waited all night for you to come here, you ain't leavin' this soon."

"Let me get this straight. You siphoned my gas so I would stop here? What is so important to tell me? What? That you can't stand the fact you were brought to justice?"

"I'm gonna call the cops," Annie protested. "And since you can't bribe them anymore they'll arrest you."

"Go call 'em. Since I'm poor that means I'm above the law, right, William? Isn't that your philosophy? Yeah, I can act like a lunatic and create havoc for all the people with money. Hey, then just like you I'll break the law over and over and proudly go to the papers and on TV and say it's justified. I'll say that because my life sucks that means I'm special and above the law. Then, I will proudly again tell everyone that I'm gonna terrorize anyone who has more money and a girlfriend. Isn't that your way of thinking?"

William stood in despair, unaware of what to say. Even if he agreed he didn't want to talk about it.

"Oh, what's wrong, William? What? Since we've switched sides you do like it that I get to harass you and get away with it? You said I know how it feels to be you; now you know how it feels to be me. You have to just put up with it. It's okay. Heck I ough'ta trash your car and justify it by saying that you deserved it for having a better car than me."

For a moment William had sorrow for Timmy and even a

realization that he was once in Timmy's shoes. Annie, being a girl and not having a full grasp on what was really going on just wished someone would grab the keys back and they could leave. She didn't care one bit for what Timmy said or thought. William did care and decided to try to talk some sense into him but realized that Timmy's perception of him might be true. Another reality set in and William knew how to respond.

"Okay, Timmy, since we have switched sides how 'bout me and my girl make out in front of you and then rub it in your face. Or maybe I can tell you how much our condo is worth and how expensive it is to live in California. I can rub it in *your* face that I have everything. Then, if you dare to piss me off I just stick my snotty nose in the air, pay off the cops and have you put in jail for crimes you didn't commit. Then I will laugh and continue my happy life not once caring about you. Doesn't that sound familiar?"

Annie went to the payphone now that William was getting into deep conversation with Timmy. She just wanted to call the cops but the payphone was out of order. The situation wasn't fully out of hand yet so she saw no reason to run into the gas station and scream for help. She figured she and William would grab back their keys and leave.

"Well, I guess you've proven your point," Timmy said. "Here's your keys. I'll let you and your little fat blond-bitch girlfriend go back to your happy life and forget all about me."

William caught the keys as they were thrown at him. He didn't want to fight with Timmy even though he made an unreasonable comment about his girl. He figured this was the end and he and Annie would talk about it for a little while when driving but then forget about it.

Chapter 4

Feel the Heat

As he looked behind him at Annie the sound froze as she screamed and put her hands on her mouth. Not knowing what was wrong he quickly he looked back at Timmy who had a handgun aimed at him.

Instantly William jumped out of the way as the gun fired. Losing his balance he fell and hit the cement. He breathed relief when he saw and felt that the bullet had missed him. As he looked at Timmy with the smoking gun in his hand the only thought was why was he smiling even though he had missed completely?

Figuring Timmy's plan was just to scare him and the miss was intentional, hence the smile, he got up. It could be possible he only had one bullet. The sound of people screaming around him was still present even though he was just fine. The screams were only because a gun had been fired. After everyone saw he was okay they would all breathe in relief.

Half out of touch with reality and really startled at this point William just wanted he and Annie to leave. He no longer cared about Timmy and trying to get his point across. He didn't even want to call the cops for the gunshot. It was clear that to just drive away and never return was the best and only choice he had.

The awfulness and complete horror was no bad dream and he saw the reason for the smile on Timmy's face. Annie lay behind him in a small pool of blood. He jumped to the ground to hold her.

"Annie! Oh God, someone please please call an ambulance." Patrons had already gone inside to call before William even said a word.

"Annie, please stay awake. You're gonna be okay."

Only grunts of nearly lifeless pain came from her. The blood pool getting bigger and bigger could only mean less and less of a chance they would return home together.

"Annie," William said, putting his hand on her wound. "Come on, you gotta make it." A small tear appeared at her eye. "Don't cr-cry," William said, having a hard time stopping the bleeding. "We'll laugh about this someday."

At this point he knew she had slipped into unconsciousness. He hoped those wouldn't be the last words she ever heard from him. As he gazed up at Timmy who stood ten feet away with a malicious look he knew once again he would "feel the heat" from the Casner/Hamlin family.

"Someone cut the phone lines for the whole station," a patron yelled. With no help on the way and no sign that anyone had a cellular phone on them William knew he must run to find a phone. A quick look around showed the nearest phone was far away and the traffic too thick to drive to a phone. Also he didn't want to just leave her there while he searched for a phone. Timmy still stood like a smiling statue.

William jumped back down to the cement to hold Annie one more time while she was still warm. It seemed she might not be totally unconscious yet but her words were intelligible. He tried over and over to stop the bleeding but with no medical help on the way yet it was a waste of precious seconds.

With a million thoughts going through his head William's first was that the phone line cutting, gas siphoning and everything else was a conspiracy against them. The only part of Timmy's plan that was uncertain was whether he was supposed to be lifeless on the cement with Annie wondering what to do.

Or was this the ultimate revenge; to hurt his one and only true love. William decided he would rob Timmy of that pleasure and help Annie himself.

After hugging her he lunged into action. Still remembering the town well he knew the General Hospital at which Mitch worked was only a mile or so away.

He lifted her up and the keys dropped to the ground. It seemed like a good plan to put her in the backseat but with many suitcases it would be hard to get her there. To move all the luggage from the backseat to the trunk could waste more precious seconds that Annie couldn't afford to lose.

He knew not to move an injured person but nobody seemed to be able to do anything. They all just stood in shock and if he left it up to the public she would just bleed to death.

Timmy, who seemed as if he knew he wouldn't put her in the backseat had already picked up William's keys, gone into the Lincoln and hit the button to open the trunk. William wondered only for a second why Timmy was helpful as he loaded Annie into the trunk. He wanted to yell at Timmy but realized that he had saved him the precious time it would have taken to set Annie down, find the keys, open the trunk and pick her up again.

Also, he knew he would have the rest of his life to hate and scream at Timmy. Right now Annie was all that mattered. He knew if he got stopped for speeding he would keep running till he got the hospital.

He would've normally been mad that the blood stains in the trunk would never come out. His classic Lincoln had been his pride and joy. When a rock hit the windshield it had ruined his day.

Now as he looked at her blood-soaked body he realized how petty the car, the condo, the money, the pride of defeating the Casners and everything else that a minute ago seemed so important had been.

He shut the trunk and ran for the driver's seat. He didn't know whether it was his mind being traumatized; he ran for what seemed way too long and still couldn't get to the front seat. It seemed the car was moving. After a quick reality check it was apparent that Timmy had stolen the car and was driving away with dying Annie in the trunk.

"Stop, you son-of-a-bitch!" William screamed as Timmy headed in a direction not on the way to the hospital. With no phones around William felt flattened and overpowered. After a new customer who had a cellular phone assured him she would call 911, William chased after Timmy.

A mile away a speeding Timmy was pulled over by Officer Rosen in a heavily populated area. Timmy was fearful of what could be found but confident it was just his speeding that got him pulled over.

"What's the problem officer?"

"Speeding, license, insurance and registration." Timmy showed his license and William's insurance card that didn't have a name on it.

"You have registration?"

"No, I musta lost it."

"You have no registration?"

"I lost the card, but I do own this car."

Rosen ran the plates and the car had not been reported stolen yet. No warrants for Timmy and the only thing wrong was just a commonly misplaced piece of paper. Timmy thought for sure he'd conned Rosen and would soon be on his way. A curious moment came about when he realized he didn't know where he was going. He assured himself that he would know what to do when the time came and it was all going to work out fine.

"Outta the car Mr. Hamlin."

"Why?"

"I said outta the car."

Timmy exited the vehicle and it seemed he didn't understand why the officer had used such an angry voice. Surely this cop had no knowledge yet of anything. He smiled and played the confused kid getting pulled over by the overzealous cop. "What is this about?"

"This car is going to be impounded for no registration. I've already called a tow truck. I just need to do an initial search."

"No, you can't search this car."

"The hell I can't. Gimmie the keys."

Before Timmy could say no, Rosen snatched the keys out of Timmy's hands. Rosen checked the glove box and the center console. So far nothing was out of the ordinary. Next he opened the suitcases. The clothes didn't trigger any alarm. Rosen was curios as to why Timmy had suitcases with some women's clothes in them. He tried to assure himself that it was just this kid's girlfriend. A quick unprofessional laugh came out as he thought maybe Timmy wore these clothes in private.

After a quick search of the inside all that was left was the truck. There was no question there was astonishment when Rosen opened the trunk.

"I need an ambulance to Fifteenth and Sunflower, requesting backup," Rosen said into his radio. Timmy was instantly arrested without a chance of an explanation. William made it to the scene quickly thanks to a police car picking him up for shouting obscenities down the street with his clothes covered in blood. Timmy was in the back of one of the many police cars when he arrived. The only sign of Annie was the huge bloodstain in the trunk and a distant ambulance siren.

"At least she's on her way to get help," William said to himself.

It worried him that so much time had passed. She had

seemed on the brink of death when he left but now the theft of his car had not only wasted precious seconds but many deadly minutes.

"I need to get to the hospital and see Annie," William said to Officer Bundy.

"Well you'll have to walk, 'cause this car must be impounded and held for evidence."

"Fine, I'll walk."

"Not so fast, William. There are some unanswered questions here."

"Like?"

"Okay, eyewitnesses said she was shot at the gas station a mile away. Then you threw her in the trunk and Tim drove away in your car."

"Yes."

"Why did you put her in the trunk? Why not call 911?"

"Timmy cut the phone lines at the station. He also siphoned my gas in a plan that I would stop there for gas. When I got there he looked like he'd been waiting a while for me."

"You really shouldn't have tampered with the evidence. We can't even draw a chalk-line now. This makes our investigation very difficult. When someone needs help you call an ambulance, not try to save her yourself."

William had been halfway to warfare before even speaking to Bundy. First Bundy had helped wrongfully convict him in the past, second was not knowing Annie's fate. Third Bundy seemed more concerned with the police work than Annie. Not even a "don't worry" or "hang in there." It seemed to William that after such trauma the cops shouldn't even be asking anything yet. Why wasn't Annie the number one thing on everyone's mind? He thought.

Bundy actually seemed pleasant mannered, soft toned, and gentle while speaking to Timmy from outside the police car.

William felt like he was the one who pulled the trigger on Timmy's girl. When Bundy returned William had only a few words for him

"I don't care about you Bundy."

"Excuse me?"

"You heard me. I don't even live here. I don't give a rat's ass about making your job harder. Annie was alive and I'm not gonna let her lay there and die just so you can have an easy day. I know you don't care, especially since it happened to me, but I do. Besides this is the easiest case ever. Timmy did it, he did it in front of lots of people with the smoking gun in his hand."

"You can cut the attitude, William."

"No, not till I see Annie. I don't care if you think I'm a punk and I don't care what anyone else thinks. All I care about is Annie. Besides how the fuck hard can this be? Timmy shot her in cold blood, first degree. He knew what he was gonna do before he did it. He did it in front of everyone, case solved! I can't believe you think that I should've just let her die so that the investigation could flow smoothly."

"Look, William, this ain't a John Wayne movie. I'd love to blow Timmy's brains out right now but we have procedures, photographs and reports we must make. Now that you tampered with it, this is going to be a harder case than it should be."

"Yeah, whatever, I'm done with you. I'm going to see Annie."

"Wait. What were you two arguing about?"

"Nothing. He waited there and when we arrived he gave some stupid speech about how I ruined his life then he shot Annie."

"Why were you and Annie out here if you live in California?"

"I needed to testify in court."

"You were subpoenaed?"

"No I came on my own."

"But why?"

"Because in the newspaper it said that they needed my testimony."

"We're not buyin' that crap, did you come out here to see Timmy?"

"No, I testified against his parents."

"You know what, I don't think you had any business out in this part of the country. You don't live here anymore, you shouldn't've been out here."

"Well, I was trying to leave but now I can't."

"Look, William, you must'a done something to tick Tim off. I can't believe he just shot her for no reason."

"He did, Goddamn it!"

"William, what is your problem? I'm trying to help you."

"No you're not. You're trying to justify Timmy's actions. I can't believe it matters. Even if I did piss him off does that make it okay to shoot my girlfriend in cold blood? I'm mad at him, do I get to shoot him because of it?"

"I just want an explanation."

"He was mad I testified against his drug dealin' parents."

"Well, I know Timmy and his parents. He's a fine young man. I just can't believe he would do this without you antagonizing him."

"You don't know him. His parents cooked meth under your nose. That's how upscale and great they are. And that's how observant you are. Look, talk to me at the hospital. I gotta get there now. Bye."

Chapter 5

Annie's Fate

William left and ran the half hour to the hospital. He arrived panting. Rather than ask the idiot at the desk what was going on he found Mitch.

"Mitch, I need to find Annie, she was brought--"

"I know," Mitch replied sternly. "I saw her come in."

"How is she?"

Mitch looked away. "Sorry, William, she was DOA. They worked on her for twenty minutes. She never had a chance, the bullet went through her internal organs."

"Where is she?" William said, trying not to sob in front of Mitch.

"The mortuary."

"I wanna see her."

"They won't let you down there, but that loose lock is still there. I'll come with you."

"No, I'll come find you later," William replied, wanting Mitch to go away because he couldn't hold in the grief any longer. As soon as Mitch was out of sight the waterworks began.

After a sneak peek at the body there was no question. With nobody looking he gave her a last hug goodbye.

"I wish I could've said something better to you before you went. I mean, my God, this was all my fault. I shouldn't've brought you. Timmy might've been aiming for me."

After sneaking back out William found Mitch was waiting outside.

"What am I gonna do?" William asked.

"What can you do?"

"I mean, even today. We were gonna go home today, it's only afternoon. I don't even know what to do the rest of the day never mind the rest of my life. Nothing will take my mind off this."

"Maybe you should go home."

"Without Annie? I can never go back to our home without her."

"Get a motel and just, I don't know, drink the day away."

"Get her outta this morgue. I want her to go back to LA."

"Okay, why?"

"Why? Because she doesn't live in this hell-hole. I don't want her buried in this place. Besides I'm sure her parents don't either." William walked away.

"Where are you going to be? I'll stop by later," Mitch called.

"Moe's Diner." While walking he had no choice but to pass the gas station again. It saddened him that his new good life had crumbled there in a microsecond, yet except for a few detectives it seemed like business as usual. "The world just keeps going without me again. By tomorrow it'll just be history," he said to himself.

"Back already?" Lois asked as he entered the diner.

"Can I have a room again?"

"Sure. I never even cleaned your old one, you can--"

"No, I need a new room."

"Okay, where's your little friend?"

"Someone shot her."

"Don't kid around. Are you two fighting?"

"No, I'll tell you some other time. Here's a couple hundred bucks."

"It's only thirty a night."

"Yeah, well I ain't goin' anywhere for a while."

"Okay, here's a key. Now, really, what happened to the girl?"

"They shot her." William laughed only for a second as he realized how ridiculous it sounded. The girl he was with a few hours ago had been shot dead less than a block away. It was no wonder Lois didn't believe him.

After three boring hours Mitch arrived. William had already spent another two hundred dollars on booze and it was disappearing fast.

"Sit down, Mitch. Have a drink on me."

"The first night is always the hardest," Mitch told an obviously drunk William.

"No, for me it's not so bad. It's gonna hit me about a month from now."

"Explain."

"If there's anything I know it's sorrow, heartache, catastrophe. At first it doesn't quite hit home. I have friends around and everyone will feel bad and comfort me while it's still fresh news. At first I'll even convince myself that I'll be okay. That I can overcome it and that Annie is in heaven waiting.

"I even try to say that I'll fully heal and move on. It takes about a month for me to know that won't happen. Everyone will stop comforting me and go back to their lives. The news and police will find a new story. The last thought of Annie will be further away. It's at this point when life just continues the way it was only without Annie.

"Ya know, it's like Annie's body. Right now it's still warm and still resembles the girl I left the hotel with this morning. I still want to be near her but before long she will get cold and stiff. A month from now I won't want to be in the same room with her."

"I get what you mean, at first it might be easier 'cause the memory of the good life is only a few hours cold."

"Yeah, like when you get out of a hot bath and into the cold. At first you have enough warmth built up to keep you going but then you get colder and colder. That's me. Life will go on without her whether I like it or not. Not only that, but I get to live with the fact it was because of me."

"Annie doesn't want you to be miserable."

"Can't help it. This is it," William said waving his arms in the air. "This is fucking it! For one brief shining moment I though my curse was over. I remember Annie once said to me that I was lucky all those bad things happened to me. That everyone has an amount of B.S. they have to put up with in life. I was lucky 'cause I got all of it out of the way before age twenty. She was wrong it's gonna be nothing but agony for me my whole life. I'm just cursed."

"I'm right there with ya. At least you had a small period of good life. Yeah, today I'm not as sad as you because I never had a girlfriend to get shot. So what's better?"

"That's a good point. I finally had the good. For almost a year I got to have a small taste of the Casner life. Or the Timmy Hamlin life. Or shall I say the normal life. Ya know? I had plenty of money, a nice car, a girl I liked, I place to live I enjoyed. But finally I had peace of mind. That burning voice that I was missing something or that I was a failure was gone. Now that's all gone and it's back. Maybe it's better to just have constant misery than have a break and have to go back. There is no question now."

"About what?"

"I really did work at Auschwitz in a past life. I really am being punished."

"Ya know, other people have lost a loved one too."

"Yeah, that's what I always hear when something like this

happens. 'This isn't anything that others haven't faced.' But how many people have as many of these things happen to them. Getting falsely arrested, I'm sure it's happened to others, and they recovered. Losing a loved one, same thing. Not having a dad, same thing. Being poor with no hope of breaking it probably happens to a few. But, having every one of them happen, very very uncommon, nothing good ever happens to me. Even if something good does happen, it gets crushed."

Mitch thought William was getting a negative attitude fast, but decided to let him feel sorry for himself.

"Yeah, well, on a brighter note, Timmy's gonna get to meet his parents in jail."

"I can't wait."

Three days later William boarded a plane back to LA. Knowing Annie had been on the plane a few days ago as well but just in the cargo area made him feel creepy. He really didn't want to go to her funeral and surely her parents were going to make it hell for him.

"This is your captain Harry Ordway speaking. We are eighty miles from LAX and will be landing shortly."

By the time the plane landed the many horrible scenarios of what Annie's family would say and do to him became overpowering. Finally, after landing and everyone left the plane he went to the desk.

"I have a return flight for tonight. Is it possible I can just take it now?"

"Well, that is the ticket you bought, but your destination isn't the most popular. What I can do is put you on connecting flights. One of them will go where you need to be. However, there is a forty-dollar fee for this."

"That's fine. I just want to leave now."

"Okay, the gate is the same and this flight boards in thirty minutes."

"Okay great."

On the plane William thought he would regret the decision, but he didn't. For the first time ever he was happy to be back in his hometown. By the time he was supposed to be at the funeral he was back at Moe's Diner in the low end hotel room. He thought he should call but then realized the family was probably playing darts and using a picture of him for the target.

Ten days after the homicide Mitch went back to the diner and found Lois. "Have you seen William? He's not answering his door."

"No, he hasn't left there in a week and he only has one more night left."

"Well, is he dead? Did you check?"

"Why don't you? Here's the key to his room." Mitch took the key and opened the door only to find the chain lock restricted full access.

"William, you in here?"

A grunt.

Mitch looked to the right and to the left for anyone observing him. With nobody looking one fierce kick took care of the chain lock.

Two steps into the room Mitch froze and muttered, "Fuckin' a, man." Fifty or more empty beer cans covered the floor along with drifts of empty cigarette packs. In a corner a pyramid made out of cans could only make Mitch shake his head. As he looked around some more he had to kick beer cans aside in order to move. It appeared the beer can pyramid was surrounded by little pyramids and what looked to be a miniature can city.

Cars, houses, buildings and a power plant all made out of cans, cigarettes and cigarette packs were the building blocks of this city. A handwritten paper sign that said "Welcome to Williamsville" and the different brands and colors of the beer cans added the perfect touch of imagination.

On the bed William lay passed out in filthy clothes, whiskers on his face and many empty boxes of Ding-Dongs, Tasty Kakes, and Twinkies next to him. Mitch grabbed the hotel ice bucket and headed to the bathroom. Intentionally he destroyed William's can city on the way. In the bathroom Mitch was amazed to see an unopened six-pack of Meisterbrew. After filling the bucket with cold water he dumped it on William. "What the?" William said.

"Hi. You've been in here for over a week while I've been working 'round the clock to get information."

"'Bout what?" William asked as he wiped water off his face.

"Timmy was denied bail and has requested a probable cause hearing for today. Him and that lawyer Miller want all charges dismissed."

"Why?"

"I don't know, it's probably a Hail Mary. Anyway Janet Cellers couldn't reach you and she asked me to find you and have you come down in case you're needed."

"I'm needed for something? Wow."

"She told me that they don't even need your eyewitness account but that you should be there just in case. I don't even think she knows why Timmy thinks the murder charges shouldn't stick."

"I don't have anything to wear to court. My nice clothes are still in my car. Oh yeah, am I ever gonna get my car back?"

"I don't know. Maybe once they make probable cause they'll give it back to you."

"Okay, I'll come down."

"There's a tailor shop a few doors down. Get some nice clothes. Ya know, ones that are *not* drenched in cheap beer, cigarette burned and Ding Dong stained."

"Sure."

In the courtroom Mitch and Riley were amazed to see a clean shaven William in a new suit and tie. With such a clean appearance only Mitch knew the real reason William was having trouble keeping his balance. A smile came to all their faces as Timmy came out in an orange prison uniform.

For a moment William felt better. He remembered when he was leaving town last year a fugitive. All he had wanted was to get the charges dropped and have some money. He had that now and as hard as it was to phantom he was actually in a better place now than when he left town originally. He didn't feel responsible for Annie's death as much and figured once Timmy got sentenced and after a few months of hard core drinking he should be okay for a while.

Chapter 6

Can I Walk?

"Next case, People vs. Timothy Hamlin, murder in the first degree."

Both Cellers and Miller were ready. The judge spoke.

"The purpose of today's hearing is to determine whether there is enough evidence to bring Mr. Hamlin to trial. Both sides will have the opportunity to call and cross examine all witnesses. Miss Cellers, you may begin."

"Your honor, I would like to call my first witness Officer Rosen."

Rosen took the stand. His slightly curly hair was gelled and properly combed. His blue suit and freshly shaven face meant he had shaved the mustache William had always remembered him having. His fit body made the suit look first-class on him. He unbuttoned the coat as he went to sit down in the witness chair.

"Officer Rosen," Judge Foster said, "do you swear to tell the truth, the whole truth and nothing but the truth so help you God?"

"I do."

"Officer Rosen," Cellers started, "could you tell me from the beginning what happened the afternoon of the arrest?"

"Yes. I observed an older Lincoln speeding down Sunflower Street."

"How fast?"

"Radar said fifty-five in a thirty-five."

"Then what?"

"I pulled the vehicle over and discovered a shaky young man."

"What do you mean shaky?"

"He was nervous. His hands trembled as he handed me his license and insurance. I asked for registration but he said he didn't have it."

"What did you do?"

"I decided to impound the vehicle. I did a quick inventory search and that's when I found it."

"What did you find?"

"In the backseat were a few suitcases but in the trunk I discovered a dead girl and a handgun. The car turned out to be recently stolen. I called for an ambulance, read Mr. Hamlin his rights and arrested him."

"Did Mr. Hamlin say anything to you?"

"Just that he wanted his lawyer, Mr. Miller."

"Did you grant that request?"

"Yes."

"No further questions." As Cellers sat down, William approached her. Despite an hour of scrubbing and buying the suit she still had to ignore the smell of alcohol that had stayed with him. "Do you need me to testify?"

"Not today, but at the trial I should. He'll probably plead out. This is a cut and dry case."

"What's this about charges being dropped?"

"Oh, this Miller thinks he's Johnny Cochran. He's just trying anything to get a good deal. I'll tell ya this will be long because they are gonna argue everything to get him a lower sentence."

"What deal do they want?"

"I thought they'd want manslaughter. I would then offer second degree but apparently he wants everything dismissed. If he thinks he's gonna hardball me he's crazy."

"Yeah," William agreed, appalled at even the idea of any charges being dismissed.

"Officer Rosen," Miller was on his feet now. "When you said my client was acting shaky, how uncommon is that?"

"Not real uncommon, but he seemed overly nervous."

"So? Maybe some are more scared of cops than others."

"I guess, but even a newly licensed teenager doesn't tremble as he did."

"So he's here today because he was trembling too much? I didn't know that was a crime."

"In itself it's not, but it's not something I will ignore. If you bothered to read the charges you would see he wasn't arrested for trembling."

"Actually it is. I mean that's the reason the girl was discovered, right?"

"It was one of many. The main reason was the inventory search I performed after impounding the vehicle."

"Did you know the car was stolen when he was pulled over?"

"No, the plates came back clean. I only discovered it later."

"After my client was arrested?"

"Yes."

"Did the insurance come out okay? Was it expired or unpaid?"

"No, insurance checked out."

"Was any other name on the insurance card that might've triggered something odd?"

"No I didn't see any name on it, just the car's information."

"What did the card say?"

"It showed that a 1965 Lincoln Continental had insurance. It had a VIN number and a policy number."

"Did the VIN match the car?"

"I didn't check it right away but later it did come back to

match that car."

"I see. So it's not standard practice to check the VIN on a car to make sure the insurance matches?"

"No, not without some suspicion that the insurance is a fake."

"So you didn't doubt at the time that Mr. Hamlin was the owner."

"I found out it was stolen a few minutes later when--"

"No, when you impounded the car you didn't know at that moment it was stolen nor did you have any reason to believe that Mr. Hamlin was not the owner of that car, yes or no."

"Objection, relevance."

"I'm trying to establish why Officer Rosen deemed it necessary to search the vehicle of Mr. Hamlin."

"The objection is overruled. Officer Rosen, answer the question. Counsel, make your point fast."

"No, I didn't know it was stolen but that wasn't why I arrested him nor the reason I found the dead girl."

"Did Mr. Hamlin have any outstanding warrants?"

"No, I ran him through NCIC and the local database. Nothing came up."

"Is Mr. Hamlin involved in any drug trafficking that you know of?"

"Not to my knowledge."

"In fact is Mr. Hamlin involved in any criminal activity?"

"His parents were arrested for operating a meth lab."

"Yes, but was he charged or in any way arrested for that?"

"No, the DA didn't charge him with anything."

"Is that the reason you wanted to search the car, for drugs?"

"No, it was an inventory search."

"To your knowledge does Mr. Hamlin even have a criminal record?"

"Not to my knowledge."

"So no prior criminal history to support him being shaky, as you put it."

"Not at the time."

"Is it too far of a reach to say that someone who has had no involvement with the law is more likely to be nervous when pulled over?"

"What do you mean?"

"I mean a criminal who knows the cops and has, let's say, drugs in the car will know how to act calmly. Someone who has had many police contacts will know what to do and say. So what I'm suggesting is that Mr. Hamlin's shaky behavior was because he'd never had much contact with the police. He was an upstanding citizen."

"I don't have immediate access to anyone's criminal record. NCIC only lists warrants and persons of interest."

"What does NCIC cover?"

"Restraining orders, sex offenders, concealed weapons permits, warrants and anyone of interest to law enforcement."

"What came up on Mr. Hamlin?"

"Nothing. I already answered that."

"Yes, well you will answer again."

"Objection, badgering."

"Counsel, tone it down. Get to the point or you will be shut down."

"Fine. Were the plates expired?"

"No."

"So insurance was clean, no reason to feel it was stolen, no warrants, no record. What was the reason you impounded the car?"

"Like I said earlier that's not the reason for the arrest."

"Can you tell me the reason?"

"Objection, asked and answered."

"Your honor, I just want to make sure we understand the

one and only reason for the search and arrest."

"Okay, Officer Rosen, answer the question but counsel you will not ask this question again. You are this close to being shut down. Move on!"

"I impounded the vehicle for no registration. Mr. Hamlin was not under arrest at that point. I did an inventory search and arrested the defendant when I discovered a dead girl and a handgun in the trunk."

"No registration, that's it?"

"Yes."

"How many people lose their registration cards?"

"I don't know."

"Do you impound every vehicle for which the driver has lost their registration card?"

"I have impounded before for no registration."

"Yes, I know. I looked up the log for you over the last three years. Last year you impounded a car for no registration. However, in that case the driver also had no plates, no insurance and no driver's license. Do you remember that case?"

"Vaguely."

"In the three years I have logs of you I have never seen you impound a car for no registration alone. However, I see a few incidents where you ticketed for no registration, but never searched and impounded the vehicle."

"I can't say I always impound a vehicle for no registration, but in this case I did."

"Officer, I also obtained impound logs for all the cops in town. In the last three years not one member of your police force has ever impounded a car that had clean plates, insurance, no warrants and the driver had a license. This is the first time this has ever happened."

"I guess I'm overzealous, but it was a good thing I was."

"This was far beyond overzealous. Especially since my client denied you the right to search the car."

"I didn't need his permission. I had already ordered the impound."

"For nothing more than no registration?"

"Objection, asked and answered."

"I just need to hear it one more time because this is the most absurd impound ever."

"Okay, answer one last time."

"Yes."

"Your honor, at this time I ask that the contents of that trunk be suppressed for unlawful search and this case be dismissed."

"Miss Cellers," Foster said, "help me out here. I need something to go with. Mr. Miller is right."

"I have an eyewitness who saw the defendant shoot this girl," Cellers replied in a desperate tone.

"Bring him up here."

William took the stand.

"William Defreno, do you swear to tell the truth, the whole truth, and nothing but the truth?"

"Yes."

William felt weird and wonderful being in the same witness chair in front of the same judge looking at Timmy. It seemed great that he would one day testify against his hated foe. This would be a joyous day except Annie wasn't watching him from the gallery and the ridiculous idea that Timmy would walk was getting a little more real.

"Mr. Defreno," Cellers started, "could you tell me what happened from the beginning?"

"I left my hotel with my girlfriend Annie. I noticed my gas gauge on empty. I had just refilled it the night before so it must'a been siphoned. I went to the gas station to fill up when

Timothy Hamlin approached us. We exchanged words and he took out a gun and shot at me. He missed me but hit Annie."

"Did you call for help?"

"Nobody had a cell phone and the payphone along with the gas station phone had the lines cut. I put her in the trunk to drive her to the hospital myself. Timothy got in the car before me and drove off in it."

"Why the trunk?"

"The backseat had suitcases in it and I didn't want to waste time moving them."

"Do you recognize the man you saw shoot Jennifer Anne Lewis?"

"Yes. It is the defendant."

"No further questions."

Miller rose.

"Did you know where Mr. Hamlin went?"

"No."

"Did you or Officer Rosen have any contact before the search of your car that day?"

"No."

"Your honor, this only proves more so that Rosen had no reason to search the car. I ask you to dismiss this now."

"Miss Cellers, I don't know what to say. I need something more. We will finish this hearing tomorrow morning."

William stepped down and spoke to Cellers. "Did I do okay?"

"Yes, but you aren't enough."

"How can that be?"

"If the trunk contents get suppressed so will your eyewitness accounts. It's called 'fruits of a poisonous tree.'"

"Explain."

"Well, without a dead body or a weapon you can't prosecute a murder. Also with no body or weapon anything associated with it is suppressed. So you seeing her dead and seeing the weapon are no good if the judge decides to suppress the evidence."

"Look, I don't know the law as well as you but how can Rosen's search be illegal? He was driving my stolen car."

"It was. He didn't know it was stolen. I'm gonna have a talk with him. He should've got a warrant or waited till the car came back stolen. He screwed up; this isn't the first time Rosen has done something stupid. A while back two murder suspects got away because he refused help from the state police."

"What are we gonna do! What are we gonna do!"

"I'm gonna have Timmy's home searched for anything he might've written down or done to put the blame on him."

"Like what? Maybe I can help."

"Like for example if he, well, I don't know, wrote it in his diary that he was gonna kill her or something like that. I'm not sure that will happen since it sounds like he planned to kill you so he probably didn't even know her name, never mind communicated in any way prior that he would shoot her."

"Anything I can do?"

"Hope the judge doesn't suppress the trunk."

The next morning a more sober and worried William arrived at the courthouse to hear the news. In the gallery were Officer Rosen and Mitch and Riley. Timmy was once again brought out in chains. William hoped this wouldn't be the last time Timmy was in chains.

Cellers began. "Your honor, Officer Rosen acted within the law. Was he overzealous? I couldn't agree more. However, that is the reason for such a low crime rate in this city. With no registration one can only wonder if a car is stolen. In this case it was and with a dying girl in the back. I believe in the Constitution and the men who wrote it. But, come on, do you really think this is what they had in mind? To let murderers go free? Where does it end? A girl was bleeding to death in the back of a stolen car. If the law can't do something about it what good are they? We might as well save the tax dollars we pay them."

"Miss Cellers, do you have any new evidence?"

"No. A search of Mr. Hamlin's home brought up nothing. The only thing I have is a hope that you will be brave enough to continue with this trial."

"Your honor," Miller said with a smile. "This was too much. The officer had no knowledge of the girl or the stolen car. He acted inappropriately. Whether we like the laws or not we have to enforce them. Without probable cause or a warrant a search of someone's vehicle is not permitted. Rosen broke that rule and as much as everyone including myself hate it you must suppress the contents of the trunk."

Rosen sat looking down trying to avoid eye contact with Cellers and William.

"Well," Foster said. "I have reviewed this carefully and both of you have valid points. If it were up to me I would easily sentence Mr. Hamlin to a lifetime of horror behind bars. But the law is the law and I must enforce it."

Foster turned and looked directly at Timmy who sat looking very optimistic for a kid in chains.

"Mr. Hamlin, may God have mercy on your soul. The contents of the trunk are suppressed. Mr. Defreno's eyewitness account is also suppressed as fruit of a poisonous tree. With no new evidence I see no reason to hold you. Case dismissed. Mr. Hamlin you are free to go."

William watched in horror as Timmy's chains were removed. Only the words "free to go" echoed in his head. Rosen sat like a zombie on the courtroom bench. William approached him.

"What are you waiting for? Someone to say 'chins up, it's

okay we all make mistakes'? Well that's not gonna happen. You more than screwed up. Timmy got away with first degree murder."

"Cops make mistakes, William."

"Yeah, but never in my favor. All the times you guys arrested me, whether you kicked the crap outta me or illegally came into another city, somehow you always justified it. Oh, but with Timmy we gotta let him go on a bad search."

"Timmy being in jail won't bring back Annie."

"No, but at least I could grieve better. Now, I gotta fight yet another personal war."

"I don't make the rules. I think Timmy should suffer as much as you do. If I hadn't searched the car we might never have found Annie. I mean nobody would know a crime was committed. I know she died anyway but at least she had a chance with him being arrested so quickly."

"Well, hats off to you. She died anyway and all you did was secure he got away with it."

Chapter 7

Personal War, Part 2

After three days, Mitch, Riley and a girl came to see William in his hotel. As they entered they grabbed the piece of paper taped to the door and handed it to him. The document contained information on where he could pick up the Lincoln. Instead of following the instructions William crumpled the paper up and threw it away.

"You don't want your car back?" Mitch asked.

"No, let 'em keep it. I can't drive a car that Annie died in. My God, did you see on the paper it said the trunk needs to be steam-cleaned for bloodstains, Annie's blood"

"When's Annie's funeral?"

"A week ago back home. I didn't go."

"Why not?"

"I don't wanna see her parents. Thanks to me their daughter's dead and nobody is gonna pay for it. I mean, they didn't call me when the paper showed Timmy free as a bird so I think it's clear they wished she hadn't met me especially when there're a million other guys she could've met and been happy with."

"You're never going home?"

"Nope. The condo is up for sale. If it sells whatever profits are left will be divided between me and Annie's parents."

"So, you're here to stay?"

"Yep, and until the condo sells I have just a couple grand, no car and Lois gave me a job working here. Isn't this a great life? I get to work here and live here. And every day when I take my smoke breaks or walk outside for some air I get to stare at the gas station where Annie died"

"Well," Mitch said as an introduction of the mystery girl who had entered the room with them, "I found this girl through a buddy of mine who likes to drive older Cadillacs. You two should talk."

"Mitch, I'm not ready to hit the hay with someone yet. Come back in a while."

"Trust me," Riley added as he and Mitch left. William looked at the woman in her thirties with blond hair, green eyes and thin build. Her jeans were old and out of style along with her K-Mart t-shirt that was too large for her. She would have been attractive if her face hadn't had bumps and whiteheads all over it and if she hadn't been so underweight. A closer examination made William decide she also looked unhealthy and in need of a good dentist.

"Hello, William. I'm Starla."

"Hi." William glanced at her again. He figured she was going to beg him for food money. Being two weeks without Annie and hanging around a dump motel made her a bit more attractive than perhaps at any other time. Still, he decided he wasn't ready to try to sleep with her but might ask to get a number for when he was ready.

"Listen, William, when I was seventeen my parents were shot in Chicago during a drive-by shooting. The boys who did it only got eleven years. They're out now, kinda like this Timmy is."

"I know how it feels," William said not wanting to talk to her.

"I bet you do. I mean, at least my guys served eleven years. This Timmy just walked and probably is laughing his ass off."

"He is."

"Well, I know you're in pain and I have a passion to help.

However, I'm broke as well. So, I would like at least a grand for my time."

William thought she must be smoking crack if she expected a grand for sex. She wasn't attractive enough even for a hundred dollars.

"I don't need a hooker, thanks."

"No, not for you, for Timmy. Mitch found out Timmy goes to this club on Fridays. This Friday I will go there and lust for him to sleep with me. I just can't live without him."

William changed his mind. Even crack wasn't strong enough to do this. He got ready to scream at her. Yet the memory of the smirk on Mitch's face made him think something good must be up with this. Then a double assurance came as he thought Riley wouldn't allow Mitch to play a mean prank on him. His interest was piqued again.

"So, you want me to pay you a grand so Timmy can get laid this Friday while I work all night? Boy, this is getting funnier and funnier."

"I only ask for the grand because I'm in such a position to help you. Plus, I can't even afford treatment anymore so you can help me as well."

"Drug treatment?" William said with a mocking laugh.

"No. My God, you can't think too well since you hooked up with a nice girl."

"Well, fill me in. I guess having a decent life made me forget how to be vengeful."

"I have AIDS, once me and Timmy boy have a hot passionate night he will too."

"You're right, I didn't think of that. See, having a break from this bullllllll- shit has totally screwed me up."

"Well?"

The thought of getting Timmy overpowered all reason. "Five hundred now, five hundred after you do it," William said quickly.

"Okay, he'll be at Teddy's tonight. You'll have to help me dress sexy."

Starla had brought a suitcase with her. After an hour of trying on different clothes she and William agreed on jeans so tight they looked painted on and a half shirt that reveled much of her upper body. She needed extra padding to help her wasting body still look healthy. She did her own makeup. By the time the sun was setting Starla looked appealing enough that William almost wanted to have her first. She looked nice enough to get attention and sleazy enough to look easy as well. William smiled that Timmy would never turn her down.

"Okay, here's your money. Come back here after it's all done."

"No, come with me. Just stay in the background."

"I guess yer drivin' cause my car's still in impound or wherever."

They arrived at Teddy's just as the last of daylight left. The parking lot was half empty, it being a weekday. The sight of a few happy couples getting in their cars reminded William of Annie.

"Okay, babe, I'm comin' in, but don't let Timmy know I'm there."

After they each got a drink and got used to the loud music and smoke in the air Starla found Timmy getting a drink at the bar.

"Oh my," Starla said, "aren't you cute as they come."

"Yeah, thanks, you don't need to tell me."

"So, how 'bout a drink?" Starla said, lightly shaking her almost bare breast in Timmy's face.

"Nah, I don't think so."

"What! Hey, I'll let you feel my goodies, big boy."

"No," Timmy said and walked away. Not knowing what to

do, Starla went back to talk to William.

"I don't know what I did wrong. The boy didn't like me."

As William was about to respond it was apparent that Timmy had spotted he and Starla together.

"Great," William replied. "Timmy saw us and now we're totally screwed."

"Sorry, William. I'm gonna go get us some drinks." As she went for the bar a keyed-up Timmy approached Starla and stopped her.

"Who's that guy you were talking to?"

"Oh, I don't know; we were just talking."

"Why talk to that loser when you could talk to a cutie like me?"

"Well, I see your point."

"This drink's on me."

The two of them sat at a booth. From a distance William watched, but didn't let his pleasure at a plan going well show. After a few drinks Timmy and Starla left together. A secret smile came from Starla as Timmy made sure they passed William together holding hands. After twenty minutes they were out of sight and William drove Starla's car back to Moe's Diner.

At nine AM a tired and worn down Starla made it back to the diner as well. A yawning William wondered how the night went.

"Sorry. Timmy's a lost cause."

"What do you mean? You two didn't do it?"

"Can we lie down for awhile? I think we're both exhausted."

"What happened?"

"Nothing. That's the problem."

"Why?"

"Timmy only went with me to show you up. But your little

Timmy friend doesn't--oh--how do I put this? He doesn't play for the right team."

"Oh my God."

"I couldn't get him to touch me." The yawning and bags under her eyes signaled that she just wanted to sleep. William was having the same thought. They slept in the same bed and even cuddled a bit.

Because the AIDS hadn't totally ruined her yet she still had a nice look to her. It felt good to sleep with a girl again even though he knew there was no chance anything else.

At two PM they awoke refreshed and aware that the plan failed.

"Look William, I won't ask for the other five hundred, but I really need the five you gave me. AIDS cocktails can cost about forty bucks a day."

"Keep the five. You tried yer best."

After she got dressed William showed her the door. Without a notion of good sense the two of them kissed.

"If I wasn't sick, I'd do you in a heartbeat."

"Me too." They departed with soft smiles on their faces.

William went back to doing the usual nothing he always did. Later Mitch and Riley made their way over. Without letting them know, he perked up because them coming over was the highlight of the day.

"We already heard," Mitch said.

"It was worth a try."

"Well, I guess you'll just have to hope God punishes Timmy, because we can't," Riley said.

"I agree. Let the forces of the universe punish those who have wronged," Mitch added. William and Riley were both surprised at such a comment. It seemed legitimate and no sign of sarcasm came with the tone. William did become distrustful when he saw Mitch hiding the last six-pack of beer under the bed.

"Well," Mitch said. "Let's have some drinks."

"Okay," William replied.

"You don't have any beer do you?" Mitch said as he secretly winked at William.

"I drank 'em all," William said, wondering what Mitch was up to now.

"Here, Riley, go get some Coors or something from the liquor store," Mitch said as he handed Riley twenty dollars.

"Okay. Wanna come with? "

"Nah, I wanna talk to William about Starla. Ya know she is a really interesting girl."

"Why don't you go buy the beer?"

"Oh, come on, we came in your truck. You really want me driving it? Besides you know I'll drink a few while I'm driving your truck back."

"Fair enough."

With Riley out of sight Mitch turned to William who had begun speculating what the new plan was. He normally would be dreading the next hair-brained idea, but not today.

"Okay, now that Gandhi is gone, with a little help from an anonymous source I know where Timmy lives and what route he takes home from Teddy's at night."

"This wouldn't happen to be the Cadillac man again? Who the hell is he?"

"You're not listening," Mitch said with a smile. "Anyway, the four of us are perfect. I've got the brains and the looks, my friend has the car and the access to materials and you've got the money."

"What's Riley got?"

"An annoying view on life. Anyway, my anonymous friend who might drive a Cadillac has sold me this little tire firework he made. It was expensive, but I know I'll be able to sell it to you and take my little cut of profit as well."

William looked at what appeared to be a cherry bomb with a tiny circuit board on it and wondered what horrible plan Mitch had. Although he shook his head in disgust and made it clear he was not vengeful regarding Timmy, there was no question he couldn't wait for Mitch to explain the plan.

"Okay, for three hundred bucks I'll sell it to you and maybe for a little more I'll help you use it."

"What? For more money?"

"Plus expenses. I gotta take a night off work and I'll need a nice dinner afterward and a massage to relieve the stress."

"What are you getting at?"

"Oh, I'm thinking one of those restaurant with like violins 'n shit; ya know, top of the line."

"Whoa," William said, putting his hands out and waving them. "Before we look at the wine menu, what the hell kinda plan do you have?"

"Okay, Timmy drives down the 58 Express after he's done at Teddy's. The speed limit is high and there is a place in the road as you head westbound that has a huge pothole. Also, in the same place the road curves and we could make sure the guardrail is not strong enough to stop a car. We can put this on his tire and with a control switch we can activate the firework just as he hits the pothole on the way home. I'll blow up the tire and hopefully he'll go right through the weak guardrail and go fifty feet below into the river."

"This is getting pretty sophisticated."

"It's perfect. His Honda is older than crap so it'll get blamed for the tire blowout."

"I don't know."

"Oh, come on, quit having to think about things. I mean, in the end you always end up doing it."

"What would Annie want me to do?"

"Annie probably is turning in her grave that you allowed Timmy to get away with murder and she probably is thanking me for helping you fight."

Riley arrived with the beer. He became concerned at his friends' ominous tone. He tossed a beer at each of them and was ready to settle down with his own.

"Okay, go put the cherry on his tire. Tonight we'll follow him and make sure it works."

Mitch got up to leave. Riley looked at him with puzzlement as to why he set the beer down and all of a sudden wanted to go.

"Ready to go, Riley?"

"I thought you wanted a beer?"

"Sorry, dude, gotta go, but I'll bet William will drink mine for me."

"I bet you're right," William replied as he grabbed the beer.

"What's going on?"

"Nothing. We were just discussing how tired we are of Timmy."

"Yes," Mitch added just before he left, "very tired." William and Mitch laughed a little. Riley's left eyebrow rose in mistrust of what the laughter was all about.

"Do I wanna know what you two are up to?"

"Nah, just know that it is mind-blowing how tired we are of Timmy. And that we would all be so cherry, oh, I mean merry if he were gone," Mitch replied.

"Hey, I don't wanna know what you're doing but just remember not to call me if you get arrested."

"Sure," Mitch replied in lightweight tone that seemed to anger Riley.

"I mean it! Don't waste yer only phone call calling me, you'd be better off calling George Bush to bail you out than me."

"I understand man."

"Sit down and have a beer now."

"Okay."

The three sat down and drank their beer. Minutes of silence went by. Nobody could think what to talk about.

"So," Riley said. "The Dodgers are coming to town. You guys should go."

"Last time I saw the Dodgers was with Annie."

"Oh, sorry."

Riley decided to keep quiet and accept the silence as they drank. When the beer was finally gone Riley was just as enthusiastic about leaving as Mitch was.

In Mitch's car, him and William sat parked near Teddy's many hours before Timmy's usual depart time. William became paranoid of two Native American girls with beads tied in their long black hair hanging out by the door of the bar. Their dark skin and identical big black eyes could easily pass them for *any guys type*. William didn't want anyone to think anything was foul.

"Mitch, I think we should find a new place to watch Timmy. I don't want those Native girls to think we're perverts waiting in the parking lot."

"Why do you care what ol' Pocahontas thinks?"

"They might call the cops, I mean come they're lookin' at me like I'm Col. Custer."

"Maybe they think I'm hot and wondering what I'm doing with you," Mitch said followed by a laugh.

"Mitch let's just stop by McDonalds across the street, we'll watch Timmy from there."

Mitch agreed and William felt healthier that it would be less suspicious and safer to hang out at McDonalds. As they sat in the new parking lot, the girls went back inside the bar and forgot about them. While they watched, Mitch got thirsty.

"I'm gonna go get a soda inside."

"Okay."

What William missed was that Mitch took his own plastic cup with him. Inside, the line seemed excessively long and he didn't want to ditch William too long in case Timmy left. After filling up his own cup with Coke he went toward the door.

One young man, probably wanting to win *McDonald's employee of the month* glanced at Mitch through his plastic glasses that fit tight around his head. With his overly dry hair that sat flat on his head like a dead beaver and acne coving his face his youthful scrawny body stopped Mitch.

"You can't fill up yer own cup," he said in his high-pitched underdeveloped voice.

"Look I already filled it, just let me go, I can't wait in line for an hour," Mitch replied thinking that with such long lines the employees main concern should be getting everyone served and not irritating him about a soda.

"Nope, you gotta dump that out."

"Oh come on, why waste it? You might as well just let me have it now, why dump it out?"

"Dump it out."

Mitch sneered at the kid and looked around to see many lights and judging eyes watching him. A smile came to his face as he awed his spectators by dumping the soda on the floor.

"There you go, dumped it out!!" Mitch bellowed with psychotic laughter. After a few seconds of making sure he absorbed all the reactions for the other patrons, he headed toward the car. William thought the running was only because Mitch didn't know Timmy hadn't left yet. The only inquiring question was where the beverage was he was supposed to buy.

"Drive!!" Mitch shouted as he got close to the car.

"What?"

"Drive the car God damn it!!"

With a tag team of employees coming out to the lot pointing toward Mitch, William decided to jump in the driver's seat and peel away fast now, then ask questions later.

After they departed the area William was ready for some real answers.

"What happened?"

"William, yer lookin' at a fuckin' hero."

"Really?"

"Yes I stood up for myself, I stood up for others, I stood up for my country."

Mitch explained with pleasure how he stood up the McDonald's.

"Let me see if I get this straight, you got caught stealing a soda and coped an attitude and think yer a hero?"

"Someone had to stand up to them."

"Ya know, you could'a said something like 'I already bought a soda, but those foam cups leak in my car so I'm just refilling it in this plastic one.'"

"Yeah, but what fun is that?"

William decided it was actually safer to stalk out Timmy in the Teddy's parking lot. As they sat Mitch and William should've been bored from waiting so long but were keyed up about the disagreement concerning McDonald's. The only thing to halt the arguing was when a patron left Teddy's in hope it would be Timmy.

Finally after almost two hours Timmy left and got in his car. A large white dust cloud came from the exhaust of the worn-out Honda. It was no secret the car burned about as much oil as it did gasoline.

The two let Timmy get a half mile head start and followed. As they made their way to the 58 Express, Timmy gained speed to 55 mph. It was easy to see the slipping of the transmission each time the car bucked shifting gears.

"Damn, he's not going fast enough," Mitch said.

"When's the turn coming?"

"In one mile and the guardrail's loose, but he hasta go at least seventy or more to break it."

"I don't know that his car can go that fast."

"Well it has to."

"Fuck it, let's go home."

As they were about to turn off a big '70s blue Cadillac with handcuffs hanging from the bumper sped past them and next to Timmy. From the passenger side of the Cadillac a very attractive young girl rolled down the window to converse with Timmy. Her long blond hair waved in the wind and the clean face and soft looking skin surprised William and Mitch as they drove two car lengths behind Timmy's Honda.

"Hey, cute boy, wanna race?"

"Nah."

"Oh, come on. If you win I'll flash you."

"Yeah," the driver added. "Come on, man, don't be a wimp. No wonder you ain't got a chick."

The girl laughed and Timmy nodded his uneasy head as he sped up. He'd never raced before and normally wouldn't care that this guy had a pretty girl and he didn't. The fact that he had come home from the nightclub alone and without money showed he had no attracting social skills. The man in the shiny big car pumped full of confidence and the trophy girl to boost his appearance made Timmy feel green-eyed for nearly the first time ever.

"What the?" William stuttered.

"Oh my God, he's been following us the whole time. Let me tell ya, he takes personal pride in his schemes."

"Who is he?"

"Who is who?"

"Come on, man, the Cadillac man."

"Pay attention. That curve is coming up fast. Here's the remote."

The Cadillac sped up just enough to get Timmy to go faster but not too much to where Timmy would give up from lack of power from the old Honda. Their speed hit sixty-five. The Cadillac slowed to give Timmy the false confidence that he could win the race. Timmy floored it to seventy-five and smirked at the fact that he had successfully passed the Cadillac. The curve was coming up fast and Timmy passed eighty while still accelerating.

"Okay, William, here comes the curve. Get ready to hit it."

With his hand on the button a flashback of when he had had Timmy sighted in his rifle exploded before his eyes. This was his second chance. Like before, Timmy's life was literally in his hands. The motive was better than before and the chances of being arrested slimmer.

As the curve neared, Mitch's eyes got bigger as he thought he would see Timmy break the guardrail and plunge into the water. His eyes squinted only to see he passed the curve without incident.

"Shit, the cherry was a dud."

"No. I didn't do it," William said, timid of what Mitch would say in response.

"What? This was perfect."

"I couldn't shoot him last year and I couldn't kill him this time."

"Gimmie that," Mitch said as he grabbed the remote and hit the button. The tire on the Honda exploded. Relief washed over the girl in the Cadillac as she thought for sure she would have to flash the kid in the Honda. With the road now being straight, the tire blowout caused Timmy and the Honda only to lose slight control and force him to the side of the road.

A dust cloud, a damaged tire and Timmy's fright were the

only casualties of the assassination stunt. As Mitch and William drove past the disabled Honda they were engaged in a heated argument. Neither one knew of the slight satisfaction that the blown tire would leave Timmy stranded all night since he had no knowledge of how to change a tire.

"William, you are the biggest fucking pussy I have ever seen. You fucking loser, you piece of garbage. You, you, you idiot, you moron, you fool, you imbecile."

William stared ahead and accepted every hurtful word. He knew Mitch was probably right, but he knew if he could do it again he would make the same choice.

They drove back to the diner. Skid marks on the pavement due to over braking from Mitch's car showed his anger at William

"Where's my three hundred bucks?"

"Here."

"Oh, and expenses."

"Here's another three hundred. Go have a dinner date with the Cadillac man."

"You had it; you could've won," Mitch yelled as William got out of the car and headed to his room.

"You don't deserve justice!" Mitch screamed as he peeled away. William went toward his room and was stopped by Lois.

"Your room needs to be repaid again."

"Here! Here's three hundred bucks for another two weeks. Does anyone else wanna take my money?"

I've spend two thousand dollars this week. That completely wipes out me and Annie's saving account, William thought. If the condo didn't sell soon he would find himself back in dire straights like before.

A week later at the early hour of noon the telephone woke up William.

"Yeah, what," a half-asleep William said.

"This is Hank from Southern California Real Estate."

"Yeah."

"I have a buyer for your condo."

"Yeah, that's great."

"Okay, they offered a little lower than you wanted but they will close fast. When can you get your furniture outta there?"

"I can't go back. Give anything good to Annie's family and trash the rest."

"That'll cost ya. It would be cheaper if you would come out here and get it."

"I'm not coming back."

"Okay, you'll still have profit."

"What are the numbers?"

"Well, the mortgage company has added late fees for three months of unpaid mortgage. Your furniture needs to be moved and my fees and paying off the mortgage will leave you with about forty grand profits."

"Okay."

"So you wanna sell?"

"Yeah. Will you do two things for me?"

"Sure."

"In the house there is a picture of me and Annie over the fireplace. We spent two days posing for it so it would be just right. Also, my dad's pocket watch in the nightstand. I want you to grab them and mail 'em to me."

"Sure. How are you and your deceased partner's family going to divide the money?"

"Tell you what, I want you to send me the picture and the watch and ten grand. Give the rest to Annie's family."

"Are you sure?"

"Yes, and tell them I am very sorry for what happened."

"Okay, will do. I'll have the papers over-nighted to you. Just sign them, return them and I'll send your personal items next week."

"Sounds good."

"Take care, sir."

"Yeah right," William said as he hung up.

Chapter 8

Back to School

At six AM a week later Riley knocked on William's door. Getting no answer he invited himself in as he usually had to do. The place had many beer cans on the floor. As he came closer to a sleeping William he noticed a framed picture of William and Annie hanging on the wall.

"Goddamn it," William yelled, half asleep. "It's the middle of the night. Come back later."

"How long?"

"Gimmie an hour."

At six thirty Riley returned. William rolled over and saw the time. Instantly his frustration rose.

"Damn it, didn't I say gimmie an hour?"

"William, it's six thirty in the evening; you've been sleeping all day." With a look outside at the setting sun it didn't take long to see Riley was right.

"Oh man."

"Weren't you supposed to work today?"

"I guess I'll hafta get fired again."

"This place smells. Do you do anything but sleep?"

"Yeah, well I've lived in a hotel almost four months. There's nothing to do but sleep. I go days without the sun. This really sucks."

"I started a semester in college. Maybe you should do the same."

"What major?"

"Criminal justice."

"Oh, how ironic."

"Tell you what, since you're nice and rested why not come down to the college tonight and check out my class."

"Oh, I don't know. I've got seventeen hours sleep today; I should probably try to hit the hay."

"Come on, don't be a smartass. Tonight we're doing speeches."

"About what?"

"Each student must do one about an issue or what they think is wrong with the justice system. They can even do a general speech about something interesting."

"Why can they do whatever? 'Cause they can't think of anything?"

"This is the first speech and the class is actually a speaking class. I think you'd like it."

"Yeah, I could give my *us*-and-*them* speech."

"What is that?"

"Oh just differences in people. Ya know some people are *us* and some are *them*."

"Um, I don't know."

"Ya know why you say that? Because you are a *them*."

"A *them*?"

"Yes, but that's okay because eighty-five percent of men are *them* and ninety-seven percent of women are *them*."

"I see," Riley said with a bothered look on his face. "Listen, just get outta this hell-hole and come to the college tonight."

"Yep a them."

"I don't know what you're talking about. I don't want to know."

"Oh, really?"

"Yes, because if you're ever back in court and I must testify as a character witness I don't want to hafta mention anything about you saying nonsense."

"Oh, okay. Did you know that Randy Casner used to wear tree leaves around his head as he stood on his roof and big brown dudes would dance around him with maracas and big bon fires and tiki torches lit?"

"No, I didn't. Is this what you think about all day? This is why you never get anything done because all that goes through your mind is stupid shit?"

"They would bow their heads down and were painted up as they all danced in a circle around him singing ouga ouga ouga chaka. You could see the flames for miles."

"Didn't know that. I hardly remember Randy Casner."

"Oh, well, downtown there's this bronze statue of Randy smiling with his hand in the air."

"I've never seen that statue."

"Oh I went and pulled it down to symbolize the fall of Randy's empire."

"Like I said, hanging around here in this dump is making you crazy."

William smiled and slowly approached Riley who could see the irrationalness in his face."

"I wanted to ask you something Riley."

"What?"

"Suppose you were to meet this new girl. She's everything you like. She's good looking, I mean real cute. She's smart, she's nice, she's got a good job and much ambition."

"Sounds good."

"You even get along real well and I mean it seems great."

"Did you meet a girl like this?"

"Well, if I did and she had all those great things but just one little thing wrong, I mean just a tiny little problem."

"What might that be?" Riley said, thinking William would say she was gay or dead.

"She shot somebody in the face."

"You met a girl like this?"

"No, but if I did I, just wanna know in advance if I should go for it."

"You really missed Mitch while you were away in Southern California, huh?"

"What do you mean?"

Because he would talk for hours about absolute nonsense like this and enjoy it."

William smiled more to the fact that someone was listening to his nonsense.

"Now, will you come to the school tonight?" Riley pleaded.

"Do you think it can be saved?"

"Can what be saved?"

"Southern California."

"What? Saved from what?"

"Ya know, just saved in general. Can it be saved?"

"Saved from earthquakes, crime, Mexicans, what do you mean?" Riley asked, realizing he had just made a mistake trying to find any logic in an idiotic and outlandish William.

"Can it be saved?" William said, followed by a snicker. Riley nodded his head and quickly dismissed the last few minutes of their conversation.

"I really think you should leave this place for awhile. Anyway, see you tonight?"

"Does the school have a bell tower?"

"You gonna be there or not?"

"What time?"

"Seven thirty."

"I'll be there."

"You need a ride?"

"No, I bought myself a piece of shit '93 Ford."

"What! Isn't your Lincoln in the impound?"

"Yeah, in fact I have thirty days to pick it up or they sell it or burn it or charity smash it or something."

"That car's a restored classic. Go get it."

"Forget it. Annie died in that car. I can never drive nor see it again. Besides I got my last ten grand to spend. I think a few months of drinking and sleeping all day should take care of that."

"Okay, please don't say anything stupid to my class, especially about this *us* and *them*."

"Maybe I can get some opinions."

"About?"

"If it can be saved."

"I mean it, if you come to my class shut up and listen."

"Hey, no problem. Don't you worry."

At seven thirty, a rested and cleaned up William appeared in the audience of Riley's class. The professor, Ms. Anderson, opened her grading book and got ready for the speeches. She reminded William of an old teacher from middle school with her curly gray hair, little glasses on a chain and thin short body. She had to be at least fifty or older with those noticeable wrinkles and sagging body. Her clothes were average and not impressive for being a college professor.

The first speech was from Michael. As he went up before the class William couldn't help noticing his appearance. Michael was a white male in his twenties who was short and at least twenty pounds underweight in comparison to most guys. His long hair, glassy eyes, undernourished body and torn jean jacket with many burns on it screamed vegetarian and marijuana user.

"Hello, I'm Michael. I hope to be a police officer. The biggest problem with criminal justice is racism. Even after over a hundred and fifty-one years since slavery we still haven't got the message. We must promote equal rights for everyone.

White privilege still exists everywhere. For example, for every dollar a white man makes a black man makes only ninety cents. Why is this true? Why can't salaries be equal for everyone?"

William tuned out most of the speech and clapped after Michael was done. Next Jerry got to do his speech. William knew he was getting judgmental but still thought out of twenty students in the class, Jerry and Riley were the only ones with the character for criminal justice. The others in the class gave off the sense of being either ex-crack-heads only wanting to be cops so they could get away with pot smoking, or delusional in the thought that law enforcement would somehow make them feel like tough guys and compensate for the fact they were easily broken.

"Hello I'm Jerry. I hope to work in corrections. What I see as the biggest problem of criminal justice is the fact that there is no second chance in the system. We live in a country where if you get too much in debt you can declare bankruptcy and start over again. Yet, in our justice system even after the punishment is served a person can never pay back his debt to society.

"For example, someone who commits a felony at age eighteen will make an average of thirty-three percent less than a non felon. Many high paying jobs require a background check. Each year the restrictions get higher and higher. Yet, according to the department of justice more and more people get arrested and acquire a record." He put up a poster board showing the steady increase in arrests from year to year.

"Twenty years ago only a felony could forbid a person from pursuing a career in criminal justice. Now almost any arrest can prevent a criminal justice job. Many jobs that felons must take are manual labor and lower paying jobs. Imagine, Ms. Anderson, if you were to take thirty-three percent of all the money you've made since age eighteen. How much would that be? What effect would it have on you?

"I would estimate by your age you have earned at least a million dollars since you were eighteen. Now subtract three hundred thirty-three thousand from that and tell me if you wouldn't feel it tremendously. I would say you might not own a house, you sure wouldn't have a job here and you probably couldn't retire.

"A felony can never be removed or expunged and will always be used against a citizen. You know, a diamond actually isn't forever, but a felony is." Laughter came from the classroom.

"Recently, it was believed that the brain was fully developed by the age of fourteen. But we now know that the areas of the brain that regulate self-control, emotions and judgment do not stop developing until as late as age twenty or even twenty-five for males. Furthermore, psychiatrists now conclude that offenders at age eighteen have a greater capacity for rehabilitation than do adults over twenty-one because they are still in the 'developmental period' and are more susceptible to change through successful intervention strategies.

"Because of their relative immaturity people eighteen have been denied much of the responsibility of adulthood including the right to drink alcohol, gamble and run for political office. Yet a felony committed at age eighteen can be used against a person for the rest of their life.

"According to the *Scientific Journal* every seven years our bodies completely rejuvenate cells. What does that mean? It means that physically what someone did seven years ago really wasn't done by them. That physical body doesn't exist. Yet the actions of that body do.

"This may only lead to re-offending. If you rob a man of opportunity you've created a dangerous person. Over fifty percent of felons re-offend, yet I can't help wondering if they tried to get into decent society but were told they simply couldn't.

"In children it has been proven that they will act the way they are treated. This means if parents continually tell their children they are 'bad' or a 'brat' chances are the kid will act that way. This is the same with adults. By never giving a person a chance to bury their past we are basically telling them they are criminals. By telling them they are criminals and treating them like outcasts for crimes committed sometimes twenty years ago it works the same; that they will act like criminals."

William paid more attention to Jerry's speech, but still wasn't amused. Once again he clapped as Riley got up to present his speech.

"Hello, I'm Riley. I work with engines but hope to get into probation or parole. Anyway, there is a burning question in the justice system, one that has been asked since the country began in 1776. Is a professional, well-trained, experienced jury better than a random jury picked from the community? Should the United States abolish a random jury of one's peers and adopt a professional jury?

"Prison is a hideous term to mention. To even suggest going to prison is a horrible frightening thought."

William nodded his head and couldn't agree more. For that second he was happy he never had to go but the thought quickly dissipated as he thought Timmy should have gone.

"Prison is a place where you learn that nobody needs you; that the outside world goes on without you. A place where friendships are shallow and even the slightest bit of luxury is considered too much for the taxpayers."

I get the point, William thought.

"A jury are the ones who can send a person to prison. Because of such responsibility it would seem fair to assume that only twelve well educated and experienced people should have that power.

"If you were on trial for murder or subject to a lawsuit that could deprive you of your freedom or of all your assets would you really want your fate to be decided by twelve people selected at random from off the street?

"Juries make up the most sensitive part of the judicial system. They decide the legal fate of the defendant and could send them to prison.

"Juries aren't perfect. Any trial attorney or district attorney can intimidate jurors with horror stories and emotion. Logically impossible scenarios, bizarre questions and strange behavior during trials can influence a juror who is unaware of the system. So who would want to be judged by twelve people off the street? It may seem that someone with a 4 year degree or higher in the judicial field would make a better juror.

"During a time when communities were closer and people cared greatly about what crimes were committed in their city a random jury was designed. In our technological, high speed society a random jury seems unneeded. Most people consider jury duty a task they wish they didn't have to do. So it would seem that random juries are outdated.

"The biggest myth is that a random jury may not be intelligent or have any idea about the judicial system. Since felons can't be jurors it's likely a jurist may not've ever been arrested nor had any police contact. People who have lived away from crime and may not have ever known of a criminal must try to fairly judge a defendant they can't in any way relate to. A common phase to describe jurors is 'twelve people too stupid to get out of jury duty.'

"So is this a jury of one's peers? Can it be fair to have a high school dropout or an eighteen-year-old be a jury of one's peers? I mean, think about it. In large communities a man who has spent his life living in the inner-city with drugs, crime and prostitution may be judged by a man who has lived a sheltered life breeding cows in the countryside and has never seen the city life. It may seem that this would not be justice. But is it?

"The judge, clerk, lawyers, DA's and even the bailiff are all highly educated professionals at their job. Yet, none of them have the power of the unprofessional jury. Is this justice?

"Yes, it can be. An unprofessional jury is the closest thing to one's peers and the best for justice. Consider that education is no guarantee of reliability or good judgment. It is overestimated that education makes a better person. Highly educated people in science, sociology, and law enforcement may lack compassion and common sense. Just because someone is smart and went to college doesn't mean they could judge a beauty contest better.

"Why should we believe that intelligent citizens have some unique capacity to separate the truth from lies? In some cases the opposite is true; smart, educated people tend to overestimate their ability to understand human nature and malicious deception. Intelligence lends itself just as freely to delusion as it does to wisdom.

"The most likely defendants are uneducated and low income. With this in mind can professional juries be fair? A career as a professional juror would probably require a four-year degree and law experience. Only one adult out of five holds a four-year college degree. So can anyone consider a panel of college-educated professionals to be 'a jury of one's peers' for the average defendant? No.

"If one out of every five jurors has a degree then yes, but for all of them to possess degrees is not a jury of one's peers. A variety is needed. Everyone from the uneducated to the extreme educated is needed to give the full fairness and truly be the jury of one's peers.

"Realize in a system of professional juries your freedom and your finances would be won or lost based upon the thoughtful deliberations of government employees. This would eliminate the right of due process. The whole idea of due process was to prevent the government from arresting and convicting citizens with no chance for complete explanations.

"The police officer and judge are government employees. It has been discovered that conflicts of political agendas may cause corruption. Example, many police agencies don't have actual quotas but a record number of tickets can be used to a police officer's advantage. If one officer writes many tickets he could be considered a hardworking and safety-oriented cop who is tough on crime while another who gives out warnings could be considered lazy and lenient on crime.

"A professional juror could be the same. By convicting many defendants or certain kinds of defendants like rapists and child molesters this could better their careers and help them politically if they run for an elected job.

"They could say something like, 'As a jurist I convicted every child sex offender I tried. I will not tolerate sex crimes.' This could help someone running for city council or a school board job. Yet, it's possible that a defendant may have been innocent in this jurist's career but he or she had to convict them to help keep their zero tolerance appearance alive. This is only one example in which a professional juror might 'tank' cases for career reasons.

"Many cities get hell-bent on cleaning up a certain kind of crime, let's say drugs. If the jurist works for the government can we say for sure that the secret policy won't be in place to make sure all drug crimes come with a guilty verdict? I say no. They only way to be fair is a random jury. What is great about our current system is that the random jury does not have their career in mind when making a judgment. A jurist will focus more on the facts because they won't have their job and financial career being at fault every time they get a case.

"But most importantly the fact that the government cannot convict someone without the public input. This random jury is the only part of the system that separates us from the King George days when a government could do whatever it wanted without public approval.

"An example is when a person fights a parking or sometimes a speeding ticket where there is no jury. It has been common to feel like the judge will never side with the person because the judge is part of the same government as the officer is. To a certain extent it is true.

"A judge may believe a cop who they might run into on a daily basis than someone they don't know. Or the fact that a city trying to generate revenue from tickets is going to convict someone who gets one. A judge's salary is paid off money generated from tickets, so why would the judge ever dismiss a case that could make the city money? Without sounding paranoid there really is a bigger motive to convict of these tickets than dismiss. With a jury of peers that feeling of government conspiracy is eliminated.

"If a professional jury is assembled it would be easier to find out their names and addresses. This opens doors to threats, bribery, and the lawyer. A person may not like a particular lawyer and vote based on counsel instead of the defendant. With random selection it's unknown who will be on a jury.

"Personal reasons can affect a professional jury. When getting the job a jurist may not have bias toward anyone. But how can we monitor them? Maybe when they start they love everything on God's green earth, but after twenty years life may change them.

"For example, let's say after ten years on the job a professional jurist may have their children killed by a drunk driver. This will most definitely change their views when the next DUI trial begins. Since this person has made this their career it's unlikely they will tell of his bias to keep his job.

"In a perfect world we would like to say that these professional jurors would be monitored to make sure they stay nonbiased. In reality, the government can't even keep track of sex offenders so it would be improbable that a professional juror would have their personal life watched to see if anything happens that would make him biased toward certain crimes.

"Professional jurors would be 'more comfortable with the proceedings.' That's bad. A comfortable juror is a juror who will make assumptions. Our system of justice goes to great lengths to ensure that juries hear only what they are supposed to hear, see only what they are supposed to see and refrain from drawing their own conclusions about legal matters. A comfortable, experienced jury may decide cases based on matters not in evidence.

"For example, in many trials the jury will never hear about the prior criminal record of the defendant. The system thinks that if a jury isn't told about the defendant's prior record it won't be considered when deliberating the case. But an experienced professional jury will know that many, if not most defendants have long prior records that can't always be admitted into evidence. Such a jury might well vote to convict a defendant based on reasonable but unsupported assumptions about the defendant's criminal record.

"Last but not least work burnouts, stereotyping or being disgusted by having to hear horrible details day after day could lead to laziness. A professional jury may find that voting 'guilty' is easier than paying attention and it gives the same result and the same paycheck. A person who has only had one trial in their life is more willing to put a hundred percent effort out and be as fair as they can. Since this may be the only trial they will ever do, enthusiasm and moral will be at their peak.

"The closest thing to a professional jury is the judge deciding the case. There is no hard evidence to suggest that bench trials yield 'better' or more consistent results than jury trials. If unprofessional jurors were unable create justice everyone would want bench trials. In fact most trials are done by a jury.

"Changes are clearly needed. Jurors need better compensation and training. Similarly, we need to make jury duty easier for middle-class and upper-class workers. Perhaps we could allow citizens to volunteer for jury duty at times convenient to them.

"Many capable people would love to perform jury duty but are never called or called when they can't participate. Juries could be permitted to play a more active role in questioning witnesses.

"A professional jury system is not an acceptable reform. In a free society, justice cannot be delegated to government professionals. In my opinion a professional jury is a step closer to a dictatorship government. It's worth the occasional poor decision or inconsistent verdict to ensure that the law cannot punish a person without the permission of twelve ordinary citizens.

"For what is a citizen if not one whose non-professional judgment ought to be trusted? And if our society trusts that judgment so little that the hardest questions of justice must be outsourced to professionals, in what sense are we still citizens?"

Chapter 9

Us and *Them*

Everyone normally would be half asleep after such a long speech. Yet William and the rest of the class stayed wide awake. There were only two more students who needed to give their speeches that day; John and Jennifer.

"Is John here?" the professor asked.

No one answered.

"Well, it looks like someone else will have to go. Does anyone else want to give a speech?"

Nobody seemed ready as Ms. Anderson looked around the room. She shuffled some papers and despised the fact that she would have to ruin a fun speech day.

"I can't excuse the class early. If nobody will go I'll have to do a quick pop quiz to pass the time."

Students moaned, but since nobody was ready the pop quiz was the only option. Everyone got their pens and paper ready and some wished they had called in sick.

"Excuse me," William said. "I feel it can be saved."

"What can be saved?"

"This class from a pop quiz."

Riley exhaled in relief that William didn't mention a certain place they'd discussed earlier.

"I know I'm not in this class and just watching, but I'd love to give a speech."

"Is it related to Criminal Justice?"

"Kinda, but more like personality types."

"Well, I guess since nobody else is ready, have at it."

Everyone clapped for William. He had saved them from a quiz but Riley seemed bothered due to the fact everyone knew he and William were acquainted.

Riley smiled and whispered, "William, what the hell are you doing?" as he walked toward the front of the class.

"Hello, I'm William Defreno and I work at a scum hole called Moe's Diner. My job there is to be the dog who gets beat. Anyway, there are two types of people; *us* and *them*."

"Oh God no," Riley said to himself, regretting asking William to come. The pop quiz didn't seem so bad now.

"Let's start with statistics. Eighty-five percent of men and ninety-seven percent of women are *them*. In other words most of you are *them*. There are different levels. A person can be an extreme or close to the border. It's not cut and dry; you could be close to an *us* but still labeled a *them*.

"Since this is Criminal Justice, I'll start with the courts. A *them* is the type who gets fair justice and accepts their fate. For example, if a *them* gets a speeding ticket they will pay it, accept it and move on with his happy life. An *us* will fight till the last man standing and Like Riley said always lose because the judge wants to steal as much revenue from the community as possible to pay their outrageous salary.

"To an *us* it's more than just money, it's personal pride, being able to fight against what is wrong. But the *them* will just pay what needs to be paid and not fight for what is right.

"In the court and community the *them* gets protected. The *us* people the law doesn't protect and always loses in court even if they are right. The *us* regrets calling the police because no matter what they always get shafted by the law. For example, if a crime is committed against an *us*, the perpetrator will get a good deal and no restitution or punishment is given to them.

"Yet, if the *us* commit even a small crime they are punished to the full extent. If they owe a debt they have to pay it. The *us* can't screw the creditors or government and get away with it.

"Then there are people who get protection and get good deals. They never have to pay a debt owed and always come out okay. They bounce checks, screw creditors and break the law often and never have to pay for what they do. They are the 'next in line' justice. They get the full respect of the law and if a crime is committed against 'em the cops will look hard and find the perpetrator. They believe in the law, because it protects them. Like It doesn't have to do with money or power; it's that these people are *them*.

"I guess next would be something like art that is something easily distinctive. An *us* likes meaningful art. Expression art with a hidden message. I guess maybe even dark art. Something that makes no sense. Yet *them* have art of flowers, mountains, sunsets and nature.

"Now as far as musicians, artists and writers; an *us* truly writes, paints or sings just for expression, no other reason. A *them* can't understand that because their motives are money and fame. A *them* can't believe that someone would put so much effort into something artistic just for expression and without a thought of money.

"Also, this may be hard to explain but only an *us* has weird picture thoughts. What I mean is they might hear something and an unrelated picture comes to mind. I don't know how to explain it but pictures, both moving and still go together with things that were said, but they may have no connection.

"Next let's move on to money. Some people acquire money. They go to college or start a business and get ahead. They get the job they went to school for and move up the ladder. They can start a business and it grows as time passes. They buy stocks and they grow. These are *them*. However a *them* can be very poor as well. The difference is how much they care. A *them* doesn't care that their poor; in fact it doesn't bother him much at all.

"Then some people never win. They can go to school, study hard, do everything right and still not get the job. If there are nine jobs available and ten people, this person will be the one who loses every time. It wouldn't matter if they were better than all nine of them, they lose. And, let's not forget that any business these people start will fail. All in all these people have a cloud, a curse on 'em. Any stock an *us* buys will crash to the ground faster than the World Trade Center. When an *us* is poor it bothers 'em. They want it all but can't have anything. They are called *us*."

Riley sat and stared just hypnotized with rage that William was in his opinion being an extreme radical, out-of-control fool even though he promised he would sit and shut up.

"Next is love. Some people meet the one they can love. It goes through the normal drama and heartaches but they meet that special someone. I don't even know how, it just does. They come along at the right time and in the right place and the right things are said and it works out. There is no way to describe it. All I can say is it works out one way or another. These are *them* people.

"Then, there are those who never hit it right. No matter what they do they always meet the wrong ones. If there were one hundred great ones and one loser they always pick the loser.

"They never fall in love and usually are always single. These are *us*. A *them* can find the love they want and with some effort actually get 'em. This is the main reason why 97% of girls are *them* because a girl can always get anyone they want. A *them* gets married usually young and lives happily ever after.

"*Us* never even comes close. They fantasize and dream of

the one who not only doesn't like 'em but probably doesn't know they even exist. An *us* never gets that dream come true and will be single for life. An *us* is independent and can be single. A *them* must have someone around. It's a good thing because an *us* is always going to be single."

Riley's stare spooked William enough to slow down the momentum, but not enough to snuff it.

"Now to sum it up more, I just want to give basic examples of the two. An *us* is an all or nothing kinda person. A *them* will plea bargain. An *us* wants to express them self. They wants their life to be an open book and everyone to know about 'em. A *them* keeps it quiet and wears a happy face. To a *them* it means nothing, but to *us* it means everything.

"A *them* will accuse an *us* of having a bad attitude or whining too much. It is only because the *them* can understand that it can't work for some. It can't work for an *us*; it's not that they don't try. If anything it's the *us* that try so hard and never win. They never taste victory.

"Another example is if something is wrong, let's say a law that is stupid. A *them* will say, 'It stinks but there's nothing we can do,' yet an *us* will say, 'what are we gonna do?' An *us* has a strong sense and very strong opinions. They'll do whatever is necessary to get their views across, even stand up in a strange classroom and make a speech. But a *them* just keeps quiet and goes along with normal life.

"A *them* is a survivalist, meaning as long as you're alive it's all good. they respect physical life and no matter what doesn't want life to end. An *us* doesn't respect the physical life but feels that if a life is miserable it's okay to end it. *Us* feels quality of life is more important than life itself. *Us* doesn't view life as such a great thing. In criminal Justice an *us* would rather fry in the chair than do life in prison, yet a *them* values life too much even if it's a lousy life.

"As for religion I guess an *us* may have a bad attitude because they can see how things really are. They don't use drugs to cover up what is real. A *them* can just be a drug addict of forget all the bad things with the squeeze of a needle. *Us* cannot and can even accept that there might be no God. *Us* is not afraid to say that God hates them.

"A *them* will devote their life to a religion that can't be proven to be true. They will believe in God even they've never spoke to him. A *them* says 'God is doing what's best for me' or 'I know God loves me and will get me through these hard times' that is an *them* way of thinking. A *them* can have bad things happen and not question it and still believe God loves them. An *us* way of thinking is not so loyal.

"An *us* demands an explanation. An *us* thinks and might say something like 'God could solve all my problems and give me a happy great life in the snap of his fingers, but instead he enjoys watching me suffer and gives everyone else a fairy tale. I bet he's got a big bucket of popcorn and views my life as a dark comedy.

A few mouths dropped along with some bolt from the blue that William spoke malicious about God.

"I see a few disgruntled faces. An *us* is not afraid to curse at God and will not accept blind love. An *us* feels God must earn their love just as he must earn his. Oh and an *us* is sarcastic. Sarcasm is an *us's* favorite expression. Yet a *them* is serious when speaking. A *them* is a cookie cutter person. They all look alike and never question life. Basically they are your normal people. An *us* constantly asks questions and explores things deep. *Us* will say something like 'before I find the answer I must first ask what is the question.'

"An *us* has amazing powers of observation. They can look at a picture and tell all about a person or a painting and decide what the artist wanted. *Us* is artistic and expresses them-self through art and music when troubled. *Them* goes to see a psychiatrist and takes anti-psychotic medication or Prozac. *Us* has no use for meds, they don't work. An *us* wants to make a statement, a *them* wants to keep quiet.

"*Us* cares what other people think. I mean really cares, while *them* doesn't. A *them* can experience a tragedy and heal through normal grieving and gets over it. A *them* says, 'Shit happens.' *Us* never says that and suffers indefinitely."

As William looked at Riley all he could see is him saying "you ass" over and over. William had no intention of giving this up.

"A *them* Joins a gang. An *us* stands alone. A *them* isn't vengeful. If you piss off a *them* they will get over it and continue even if wronged. A *them* believes in Karma and feels that fate punishes those who wronged him. An *us* is vengeful and believes Karma is too busy and if you want justice, you must get it yourself. You won't want to piss off an *us* because long after you have forgotten about them, they will still remember you. Just remember an *us* never forgets!

An *us* is curious, they want to know what's really going on. Maybe like if there are such things as aliens or other life. Or maybe what really happened in the many conspiracies of the past. A them doesn't care unless it directly effects their life, they are not curious at all.

"In history there are many examples of *us*. Good and bad. I mean everyone from Martin Luther King to Timothy McVeigh. These people saw problems and did something good or bad about them. They didn't just find paradise in America like everyone else.

"To sum it up the best characteristic of an *us* is that they have great passion for what they do. They are unique and are strong hard willed people. They've had it so rough and battle all they way and usually never give up. They are there when you need 'em.

"The best characteristic of a *them* is that they don't need to fight for anything because life easy. They don't care about the big picture and are ignorant. But hey, ignorance is bliss. *Them* has it easy and is happy. Sadly the *us* population is going down all the time; a dying breed. But the *them* is happy of that because they want the *us* to go away and not ruin their happy little lives. To sum this all up it's a *them* that you wanna be and since most people are *them* I guess life only sucks for the few *us* people and--"

"Okay, William," Ms. Anderson interrupted, "your time is up. I found it, well, I don't know, I guess bizarre, but interesting."

"Oh, I've just touched the surface."

"Oh, you're wrong; you're done."

William sat down as everyone stared at him. He didn't know whether they thought he very intellectual and far beyond what they could ever comprehend or just a nut. He also didn't know where he fit in at this point. An *us* would care deeply like he did about what everyone thought, yet like a *them* he had given in easily when the speech was cut short.

Riley was glad it was over as he sat stiffly in his chair. He had been about ready to yell "time's up" before Anderson did. Everyone knew he was the one who had brought in William and now would be judged fanatical by association.

Next came Jennifer. William nodded his head at this perfect looking college girl. Her smiling face, long blond hair, tight body and light blue eyes were a flawless exterior that made William decide she had never suffered a day in her life. She probably had liberal rich parents who were paying her college tuition, a healthy mental state and a parade of boys worshiping her, lusting to get in her pants. She was without question an extreme *them*.

"Hello, everyone, I'm Jennifer and I hope to work with children someday. My question is; why do we kill people to show that killing people is wrong? Why can't every state abolish capital punishment?"

William dozed into dreamland. He thought that being a single guy of course he should talk to her when she got done. Then he reminded himself a perfect girl like her sure wouldn't want an embittered and troubled person like himself. He though he would go up and introduce himself as Riley's friend. Then he realized she would just say, "Oh really, Riley's friend. Oh forgive me, I just thought you were a nut."

Since she had a fairytale life there would be no chance she would want to hear five minutes of the trouble he had. William wondered why she even bothered to go to school. Surely some rich guy would marry her and she could stay home and max out his credit card all day instead of doing homework.

He awoke from the daydream as Jennifer put up a poster board of what offenses were executable for state and federal crimes. William's rage kicked up a notch when he saw that murder was a state crime punishable by death. It seemed he was the one whom was sentenced to death, not Timmy.

His mouth dropped when she put up the offenses under federal crimes.

"Kidnapping resulting in death" was not only a federal crime but one punishable by death. William became inquiring about this crime. After she was done the floor was opened to questions. Since William was already branded a nut he decided to further make a dupe of himself.

"Yes, you in the back, um, the us and them guy," Jennifer said.

"Yes, I'm actually William, anyway do you think they should bring back the chair? I mean this pussy injection they do just doesn't do justice. Me personally, If I ever had to be executed I would wanna ride the lightin' what do you think?"

Jen become baffled at the question since her whole speech was about ending capital punishment.

After clapping for her the class was over. A stare was all William needed to know he didn't want to approach Riley; it seemed he should let him cool down for a while.

The next morning William went to the police station nice and early. He approached a woman in her forties with puffy brown hair. Her body was thin and she wore what seemed to be a man's business suit. Her face contained a huge contrast from her pale white skin to her dark red lipstick. She must have been bored since her long red fingernails tapped the marble counter. As William approached he smiled at the smell of her expensive perfume but was troubled by the smirk on her face that screamed attitude problem.

"How can I help you?" she asked in an eastern accent. William slightly laughed at her squeaky annoying voice.

William couldn't help but notice the diamond ring on her finger that was almost the size of a marble and sparkled in the well lit corridor of the police department. He stereotyped that some fat, hairy, greasy Italian guy with a suit 'n tie from New Jersey probably spent as much as a new car to give her that ring and secure her devotion to him through sparkles.

"I need all the police reports for the Jennifer Annie Lewis murder. It happened April tenth, and the names Timothy Hamlin and Officer Rosen should be in them."

"Police reports aren't free you know."

"That's fine."

"Well, a murder could have several pages and it'll get expensive," she said, smacking her sugarless gum.

"Luckily I work at Moe's Diner so money is not an issue."

"Well, we only take cash and it's gonna cost ya plenty."

"Here," William said, throwing three hundred dollars on the counter. "Please just get me the reports."

She went to get the reports but had to stop to talk about how cute the gold bracelet her co-worker wore was. After thirty minutes she returned to the area where William was getting tired of sitting on a wooden bench staring at the wall.

"Sorry, sugar, there're no police reports that match any of those names or dates."

"What, it was a murder. There's nothing?"

"Nothing sugar."

"Oh my God, how can that be?"

"Sorry hon."

"Well, thanks anyway toots."

"Bye."

William went from the station to Mitch's house. The whole time he thought, *what could've happened to those reports?* She must have just not looked hard enough.

"William, Riley told me about the speech you gave."

"Is he still mad?"

"Nah, he just thinks you're a lunatic."

"Join the club. Anyway, I wanted to get the police reports for Annie's murder and they're gone. I mean no reports, photos, it's like it never happened."

"Did you ask Rosen why?"

"Oh, he won't know."

"You know what I do know?" Mitch asked with a raised eyebrow.

"What Mitch?"

"I know where Rosen lives and for a hundred bucks you can too."

"Okay, here," William said, handing him a hundred dollars without a thought of the unreasonableness of it.

"2398 West 3rd Avenue."

"What good will that do me? You just got me to waste a hundred bucks, asswipe."

"Well, for another two hundred I'll tell you what good it will do."

"Forget it!"

"Come on, me and a friend of mine stalked Rosen out. I mean we know the truth and you can too."

"You can't just tell me?"

"We put in long hours, boring hours, to find this out. I need some compensation."

"You're a punk mother-fucker," William said as he handed Mitch two hundred more dollars.

"Okay, great investment. We saw Timmy visit Rosen several times."

"Why?"

"Don't know, but that's probably why the police report is missing."

"Wow."

"Hey, I got a new plan to get Timmy. All we need is some fake corpses and--"

"Forget it, I got my own plan."

"Okay, but if you come crawling back later I'm doubling the price. Good ideas appreciate in value ya know."

"Hey, Mitch, do you think it can be saved?"

"What?"

"Southern California."

"Well, there are many things to consider. I mean anything can be saved; it's just who will do it and how much is it worth. I would say it has a lot of value, but can it be saved cheap? I say no, but I feel it can be saved. Now also consider that--"

"I hafta go, but save that thought for Riley. He has been very interested in this subject," William said, realizing he had just got a taste of his own medicine by having to hear Mitch ramble on and on about nonsense.

William left Mitch's house. "My God, and Riley thinks I'm a nut," William said to himself amazed that his whole three hundred bucks had been extorted from him. After returning home he waited for the sun to set and went out again.

Chapter 10

A Chat with Rosen

At Officer Rosen's apartment the atmosphere was tranquil; a few empty cans of beer, the police uniform on the floor, an airplane movie on the TV and Rosen sitting on the sofa in a tank top and sweatpants with his feet on the table. The only thing to disturb the harmony was a noise from the other room. He got up, looked around and decided the coast was clear.

As he was about to sit back down a force threw him down. He looked up only to see a man standing above him with a gun.

"Sit down, dammit!"

"William Defreno, how'd you find me?"

"Shut up. Tonight you answer my questions," William replied, sticking the gun three inches from Rosen's face.

"You gotta be kidding me. Are you still mad about my mistake? If you only knew how sorry I was."

"Sure you are. Why are the police reports missing?"

"I don't know."

"I'm gonna kill you anyway and search this place till I find 'em so you might as well just tell me the truth."

"They're in the desk in my bedroom."

"Here," William said as he handed Rosen a pair of handcuffs. "Handcuff yourself behind your back." Rosen did as he was told and William watched to make sure the cuffs were secure and nothing tricky could happen.

His hope was William would be gone long enough he could find his gun but William returned shortly with the reports and several crime scene photos.

"What the hell is going on William?"

"Why don't you tell me? Why are you hiding these reports and photos?" William said, sitting on the chair across from Rosen on the sofa. As Rosen went to stand up thinking this was nothing to be alarmed about William aimed the gun at him as a reminder of who had the power and signaled him to sit back down.

"I wasn't hiding them. Besides, what good are they to you? Even if Timmy confesses to the newspaper he can't be charged with Annie's murder. He got away with it and you're only gonna get yourself a jail cell if you keep trying to bring him down. It was a horrible mistake."

"Then why hide 'em if they're worthless?"

"I took them home to study them. I wanted to see if there was anything I could charge Timmy with. Even if it's something small I want to see him charged. Every night I think about it. I even wanted to charge him with cutting the phone wires or disturbing the peace. I mean anything is fine. I even wanted them to not plea bargain his traffic ticket. I'm out to get this kid."

"Do you think about it with Timmy? Why is he over here so often?"

"So is that you in that Cadillac that keeps parking across the street? I know when I'm being watched."

"Just shut up and answer."

"How can I answer if you want me to shut up? I can't do both."

"I would not advise being a smartass right now."

"Better than being a dumbass like you."

"You know, you're pretty cocky for someone who has a gun aimed at his face."

"Because you're a fool. I'm on your side. I'm on the law's side. You may not think I like you, but even if I don't I took an oath to protect. Timmy hurt everyone in this town by getting away with a crime. What's with you? Get this through yer skull; it's not just you versus the world. It's team effort."

"Sure. You're as crooked as Timmy and his family."

"I mean it. If you only knew how stupid this is. Besides you wanna talk criminal, you break into my house, handcuff me, steal my stuff, threaten me and aim a gun at me just because I made an honest mistake. I'm doing all I can to correct that mistake, but you can't just let me work. I hope you know that those are the original copies of the reports. If you lose them they're gone forever. That's why they're safer with me."

"Are you gonna tell me why Timmy comes over or are you gonna give me more lies and bullshit?"

"I invited him over just to chat since he's without his parents. I think he thinks of me as his friend since I made the mistake. Timmy talks for hours to me and I just listen."

"Why? You wanna make him feel better?"

"No! Although I try to be supportive I'm hoping he'll say or do something so I can charge him with a new crime or maybe a Hale Mary that he'll say something that could get the murder charges re-filed without a weapon on body or eyewitness accounts. He has no idea that I'm just looking for a reason to get him. Of course if I tell him that he'll stop talking to me."

"What does he say?"

"So far just crap about his parents, but as he trusts me more and more I know I can get him to slip up on something. In fact just between you and me I actually in a way encourage him to commit another crime. I mean not a murder, but something that won't hurt anyone and then I'll grab him.

"Ya know I make him feel cocky that he got away with it once hoping he'll think he can commit anything he wants. I even nick named him 'Teflon Timmy' because nothing sticks to him, but I hope to rename him 'Velcro Timmy' someday.

"Even though he can't be charged with murder if he commits another crime it can be admitted into evidence that he was arrested for murder but got off on a technicality. Heck, any jury will fry him for anything after hearing that."

"Oh, and why share this great secret with me?"

"I'm sure in your screwed up head you think we're plotting some conspiracy to bring about your demise. But since you were the only victim in this town of this crime I feel you should have an insider on what's being done. Plus, knowing you, I'm sure you won't tell anyone."

"Hey, why not conspire to bring me down? You've done it before."

"That was Marshall. He's dead."

"Here's the handcuff key." William threw the key to the other side of the room. "By the time you're un-handcuffed I'll be gone."

"Oh good. Please be careful with those reports. You don't understand just how badly you're fucking up this case by doing this. Me being friends with Timmy is our only chance. I need those reports to study. You're undoing all my hard work."

"The case is already fucked."

Rosen laughed and realized William was going to take the reports no matter what was said. "I'll bet you think you're a real hero, huh William?"

"I never wanted to be, but living here I have to be."

"Oh God, you just can't give up till you go to jail, huh? I mean even with the Casners. If you'd just stayed out of it and let the police handle it you would've never had so much trouble. But for some reason you just think you're smarter than everyone and that everything is a conspiracy against you. You just never quit, huh?"

"Nope, I guess I must be an *us*," William said as he left.

"An *us*? I'd say an idiot is more like it." Within twenty minutes Rosen had un-handcuffed himself. It was clear William was long gone with all the reports. Rosen shook his head and went back to watching his airplane movie.

The next morning six officers showed up at Moe's Diner.

"May I help you?" Lois asked.

"Where is he?" Rosen, who seemed to be the leader of the posse asked.

"Who?"

"Goddamn it, William Defreno, where the hell is he?"

"He's in 101, but he--"

"Thank you. Move outta the way."

"Wait, is he in trouble again?"

"Isn't he always?"

Rosen and the gang went to room 101. Rosen straitened his uniform, put on an angry face and double-checked that his handcuffs were in their place and properly working.

"Here's the keys," Lois said, trying to keep up with them.

"No need," Rosen replied as he revealed that the crew had a battering ram. With a nice hit from two officers the poorly constructed door crumbled to pieces. Without letting the dust clear Rosen went inside and signaled the other five to stay back. With his night stick swinging in his hand he seemed blissful as he looked around. William's clothes and many personal belongings were still there, but no sign of him.

"William! Get out here, now! Come on, come out, come out wherever you are."

Lois caught up to them and said, "If you'd just listen before destroying my place I'da told you he got his paycheck and said he was going to check out tomorrow. "Where'd he go?"

"Don't know."

"What car does he drive?"

"That black Ford."

"The one we passed in the parking lot?"

"I don't know. Was it black and shabby and the paint was oxidized?"

"Yep, that's the one in the lot. He's on foot. What's he wearing?"

"I don't know. I wonder why he didn't take his car," Lois replied. Even though once again William had brought the police over to harass her and destroy the place she hoped he would get away.

"Wonderful. Well, we'd better go."

"Attention all units, we have a white male on foot, unknown clothing. His name is William Defreno. He is armed and dangerous and a flight risk," one of the officers said into the police radio.

The five cops headed for the door. Just out of irritation Rosen smashed a lamp by the door as he left the motel room. Lois didn't follow, instead went to see just how much damage was done to the door. One glance suggested not only a new door, but new jambs and framework would be needed along with a new lamp.

"Rosen," Lois yelled.

"What?"

"If you do see William, you tell him he's fired."

As the officers got to the parking lot a black Ford left tread marks as it peeled away. All he had time to take with him before the cops broke down the door was his wallet, the picture of Annie and him, dad's pocket watch and the reports. The six cops had taken only three cars and two were parked at the back of the building. Without thinking Rosen took the police car closest and told the other five to pile into the other ones.

"I'll tell you where I'm at. He won't get away," he said as the others walked to the back to get the other cars.

Rosen floored the car to the limit and didn't take long to catch up to the feeble Ford. Rosen's lights and sirens went on, but it was unmistakable that William had no intention of stopping. Rosen crashed into the back of the Ford, spinning it out of control and the car ended up breaking a white fence and stopped on someone's recently watered front yard. Rosen passed the house since he was moving too fast and needed to turn around to catch up.

William floored the car only to see he was just digging a trench in this person's yard. After spinning the car's tires for almost twenty seconds he was frying the engine and Rosen had caught up to him. After ruining the grass completely, driving through the person's backyard and filling the air with the smell of burnt transmission fluid, William crashed through the back fence of the property and was back on the road.

Rosen's car had trouble with traction as he went through the same muddy mess to catch up. The grass he needed for traction was used up and the pure mud and deep tire tracks bogged down the police car for the thirty seconds William needed to get a head start.

William was just about to call it quits as his old Ford was losing even more power and one glance in the rearview mirror showed Rosen had just crashed through a different part of the residence's backyard fence. With mud spraying like crazy from the back of the police car and the road being straight it would be only seconds before this chase was done.

The most wonderful sound ever came to William's ears; the sound of the train nearing traffic up the road. The wigwags were down and the crossing lights were flashing. The train itself though was still a good hundred feet away. William floored the car and heard the train's whistle along with the clanking gears of his burnt transmission.

William illegally passed two cars waiting at the crossing

and was single-minded on making it through the crossing. The train whistled over and over as the panicked engineer slammed on its brakes. The train slowed down as William's car sped up just enough to avoid collision and close enough so that it was perilous for Rosen to try to duplicate the outrageously dangerous stunt.

"Goddamn it!" were the only words said as the other police car occupants asked about the progress of the chase via the radio.

Chapter 11

Help from Above

After two days a dirty, unshaven and tired man appeared at the local FBI branch. Grime on his face, dirty torn sweatpants and sweat-stained and stretched white shirt had him sticking out like a sore thumb among the men and women in business suits. "Can I help you?" the secretary asked, thinking this man was a derelict.

"I have an appointment to see Agent Mahoney."

"What's your name and when did you make the appointment?"

"Two days ago and I'm William Defreno."

"He's at lunch, but will be back shortly."

William sat in the lobby waiting. Even though he knew he was wanted he didn't hide his appearance in any way. Every time the door opened he thought it was either Mahoney coming to maybe help him or Rosen looking for him to fry him.

The artwork on the walls was amusing. One of J. Edgar Hoover and another of a scared little girl hugging a police officer's leg. These and the fine Ansel Adams portraits, photos of Republican presidents and many historical landmarks from Washington D.C. attempted to imbue an atmosphere of high law enforcement. Many wanted posters with a red stamped "captured" across them filled the other wall. William wondered whether his wanted poster would soon have the same word stamped on it.

"William Defreno?"

"Yes."

"Come with me. I'm Agent Mahoney."

They entered the office and closed the door. Mahoney at six feet tall with clean shaven face and spiked gelled hair played the part as William had expected. The agent took his gun out of his blue suit and set it in his desk.

A moment of fear descended upon William for no other reason but that this guy was powerful and his expression and movements seemed to indicate he could get him to confess to the Kennedy assassination if he wanted. He sat down, rolled his chair close to his desk, put his hands together on the polished wood surface and said, "So, you're William Defreno?" His two pointer fingers pointed at William and his head slightly nodded as he contemplated that this tattered man was not the image of the 'Casner conqueror' he had estimated.

"Yes."

"You're the one who sent the anonymous letter that busted the Casner meth lab and the corruption of Officer Marshall," Mahoney asked in his deep sinister voice.

"Yeah."

"Also your girl was murdered by the Casner son and the case was dismissed."

"Yes, her name was Annie."

"I know. You told me over the phone two days ago."

"Oh yeah, that call just seemed so long ago."

"I also hear you're wanted by the local authorities."

"Probably."

"There's no probably about it."

"I agree."

"Ya know, if I were doing my job I would arrest you now and hold you till they come."

"Would you look at what I have first?"

"Sure," Mahoney replied, leaning back in his chair.

"I have the police reports for Annie's murder. I figured it

was a long shot and I normally wouldn't've come, but the fact that the cop Rosen who was the one who let the killer free was the one who stole the reports got me suspicious."

"Is that what this warrant for you is? All I know is you broke into this Rosen's apartment and threatened him."

"Yeah."

"Has Rosen tried to arrest you for this yet?"

"Yes."

"Oh okay."

"You didn't know about the car chase?"

"I just wanted to know if *you* knew," Mahoney said with a smile and a chilling stare in his eyes. William became petrified as Mahoney just kept staring at him with a smile for many moments of silence, still he continued with what he set out to do.

"I have lived in the town for a while. I'm not just being paranoid when I say there is a great deal of corruption there."

"Why'd you take the reports?"

"I realize this was kinda stupid, but I had bet Rosen had never asked if anything Timmy did was a Federal crime. I figured you guys never even got the reports."

"No, actually this is the first the FBI has heard of this."

"I just wanted you to look them over. Since no state crimes can be any good, maybe see if any federal charges can be brought against Tim."

"Okay, well, come back in an hour or so and let me look at these reports in quiet."

"Okay."

"Maybe clean yourself up a bit, huh? You smell awful and your clothes are full of grass stains."

"Oh yeah."

"Where'd you sleep the last two nights?"

"In the woods the first night, but last night I slept in the

Winchell's bathroom."

"How terrible."

"Nah, I ate doughnuts and drank coffee all night. Nobody ever comes in the bathroom."

"No money for a hotel?"

"I got plenty of money, I just figured every hotel in the county was gonna get searched looking for me."

"You're that important, you think?"

"You don't know Rosen. He will stop at nothing to grill me."

"My God," Mahoney said, not knowing whether William was a victim of a corrupt overzealous police tag team or just a mentally unstable criminal. Mahoney figured since he had come in voluntarily, either way William would come back to him and it wouldn't be necessary for restraints to be used. "Just give me an hour."

"Sure."

William went to his car and got out some money for new clothes. The local K-Mart had cheap outfits on sale. Before going in he noticed a Men's Warehouse about the same distance away. Since he figured it was only a matter of time before he was in a jail cell he went inside the Men's Warehouse to buy better clothes.

On the way back he bought some Starbucks coffee from a vending cart. In the bathroom of the FBI office he locked the door and took a quick splash bath using the sink.

The bathroom had marble sinks and soothing dark painted textured walls along with un-cracked ceramic tile along the floor and as high as the sink. The nice smell and sparkling surroundings made William feel a tad guilty as he used the fragranced hand soap all over his body and made a mess of water on the floor. With freshly washed hair, nice smelling cologne and a new suit and tie he emerged and approached the secretary who asked, “Can I help you?”

“I’m William Defreno. I’m just giving Agent Mahoney some time.”

“Oh, I’m sorry,” she replied, embarrassed cleanliness had changed him so much she thought it was someone else. William got flustered when he saw two police officers arriving. Had Mahoney called them and just stalled him till they came?

A split second decision was made not to try and run. Mahoney was his only hope and if this was a sell-out there was no one else to run to. William would accept this was the total end and not fight the arrest. The two cops walked by and seemed to have no interest in him whatsoever. William laughed and reminded himself he was an untrusting person.

“All right, William, come on back,” Mahoney said.

“What do you think?” William asked as they sat down. Mahoney didn’t sport the same bulldog demeanor and chilling expression he had when they first met. He actually smiled at the sharp charcoal suit and blue tie William had bought.

“Okay, as far as arresting this Timothy Hamlin for a federal crime we have a problem. Here’s what I found.”

“What?”

“From your eyewitness account and these reports he was aware Annie was in need of urgent medical care. Yet, knowing this he stole the car with her in the trunk. He also didn’t head to a hospital and never mentioned her urgent need to Rosen when he was pulled over.

“Now, of course he can never be charged with shooting her or stealing your car; those are state crimes and he was cleared of them. But kidnapping a person who is in need of urgent medical care and especially when the perpetrator knows this can be Federal kidnapping.”

“But what’s wrong?”

“He can only be charged with Federal kidnapping resulting

in death if we can prove Annie was still alive when Tim stole your car. She was DOA so it's almost impossible to know whether she was still alive at the moment Tim stole the car. Without concrete poof all that would be is stealing a dead body which is state and he's been cleared. You see what I mean, yes he did kidnap her, but if he killed her before the kidnapping then that's not kidnapping and there is nothing we can do. Also she never showed any affection for Timmy?"

"No, why."

"I just want to make sure that there was no way she would willingly go with him if she had a choice. Also, these reports prove he knew she was in the back, but she had to have been breathing with a pulse for it to be kidnapping."

"Hmm, really? How can I prove she was alive?"

"Well, we could look in your car, but after this much time I'm sure everything's been cleaned up and is too tainted to be proof."

"No!" William said so loud that it startled Mahoney. "I felt so horrible after her death I never even picked up the car from impound. It hasn't been touched in all these months."

"It hasn't been cleaned out or driven since the crime?"

"No, but I'll bet the impound fees are high."

"You never went to get your car back?"

"No, in fact the police never really checked it out. It was impounded and inventoried, but since Timmy got away with it, it never got combed or anything."

"I hope they haven't auctioned it after this much time."

"No, two weeks ago I actually got a letter saying that I only had another thirty days or it would be sold. Also that there was blood stains in the trunk. So it literally is just like it was when it happened."

"Okay, I guess it can't hurt to have a look at it. I'm glad you preserved it all this time."

"Well, I think I more like procrastinated."

They drove to the impound lot in Mahoney's government issued black Crown Victoria. The tinted windows made the ride pleasant on a day with such sun glare.

"Hello," William said to Barry, the impound manager. "I'm here to pick up 88094."

"Oh, I'd say it's about time you showed up. We were gonna auction this thing in ten days." Barry was the bearded, typical hairy overweight good ole boy William had expected to see.

"Just in time then, huh?"

"Yep, you owe us nine hundred and fifty-two dollars in fees."

"Oh my God."

"Yeah, pick your shit up on time."

"Excuse me," Mahoney interrupted. "We would like to just look at the car before we pay."

"Sure, but you ain't getting the keys."

They went through the rows of impounded cars. The Lincoln was near the back since it had been there so long. William's legs felt like jelly and his stomach tingled at the thought of having to see the car again. He had thought he would never have to see it again and especially since it hadn't been touched since that horrible day.

"Okay, can we just have the truck key?" Mahoney asked the man.

"Sure. Are you gonna pick this thing up today or not?"

"Yes." Barry walked away satisfied.

Mahoney opened the trunk. William just couldn't bear to look at the last place he had seen Annie.

"I'll be right back," William said as he walked toward the bathroom. He did not want Mahoney seeing him so devastated by this. After ten minutes in the bathroom William had hyped himself up enough to look in the trunk and be of some help to Mahoney.

Back in the yard he found Mahoney on his cell phone and Barry handing him a sheaf of recently faxed documents.

"Yes," Mahoney said into his phone. "We'll bill him later for the impound. I just wanna get this car outta here and get a crew on it. I don't have my camera on me, but I got the reports, thank you." He snapped his phone shut.

"What's up?"

"Well, it looks like I can get a crew on it. Let's look and see if anything can prove Annie was alive, but don't touch anything."

William went to look inside as if he was just looking at any crime scene, blocking out in his mine his relationship to this one. Before he bent to get a view, however, Mahoney stopped him.

"Look, William, I need you to sign this car over to the FBI. I don't wanna wait to get it seized because if you're right about this Rosen wanting to cover it up I don't wanna lose this. Plus with probably no proof the FBI probably wont pursue this unless we make it easy to get access to it, I mean they're being quite kind doing this."

William nodded and gave no indication of ingratitude or that he didn't want to sign the car over.

"You were right this car hasn't been touched since it happened. Your suitcases and rotten food is still in the backseat." Mahoney said as he handed William the release form that had been faxed.

"You think you'll find something?"

"No, but I pulled some strings and at least got a crew to look at it. Don't get too excited. We have a long way to go. So far I see nothing but maybe a close examination will prove something. Yer lucky, I only got them to look at it because it literally is just like the day it happened."

"You have a pen?"

"No, um, let's go get one from the office. Oh, and after this is all done the FBI will bill you for the impound fees."

"I don't care."

Chapter 12

A Familiar Place

“Okay William, let’s go,” a voice said from behind them. William turned to see Officers Rosen, Bundy and Beckworth with their night sticks out and handcuffs in Rosen’s hand ready to be used.

“Okay, I need to sign this then I’ll go.”

“Now!” Rosen barked as he threw him against a car. William’s hand went through the car window as he tried to stop himself from falling.

“What are you doing here?” Rosen asked.

“Excuse me, I’m Agent Mahoney of the FBI. We’re looking at the car used in the Annie Lewis murder and we have requested a crew to look at it.”

“Well that car’s still in police impound and since its owner is going straight to jail it is therefore in our possession. We’ll give it to you after we’re done with it.”

“Afraid not. The owner has signed it over to the FBI and the fees are being paid,” Mahoney said as he handed Rosen the unsigned release.

“No, he didn’t sign it. Besides what business is it of yours? Boys go get Barry.”

“You’ve had all these months to look at it Mr. Rosen. Why all of a sudden when my boys would like to look at it do you now want your boys to look at it?”

“Like I said this in not an FBI issue; go fight some white collar crime somewhere in New York.”

One of Barry’s clerks showed Rosen that nine fifty-two

needed to be paid to release the car. Before Rosen could respond Barry came out and informed everyone that no fees needed to be paid. Mahoney only nodded his head that Barry would charge the FBI the fees, but some small town cowboy cop got them waived.

"No, don't let Rosen get his hands on the car," William shouted to Mahoney.

"Shut up man! Shut up!" Rosen replied.

"You have to sign this," Mahoney said in disappointment that it was apparent Rosen was not going to let William sign over the car. William was fuming that he hadn't had a chance to sign the paper. As Rosen went to handcuff William he stopped at the sight that William's wrist was bleeding.

"You have a bandage?" Rosen asked Bundy. Normally Rosen wouldn't care about bleeding, but wanted to look as professional as possible in front of a higher law enforcement officer.

"Yeah, I'll get it." Rosen turned away for just a split second, long enough for William to jab him and break free. In the twinkle of an eye William had snatched the paper out of Mahoney's hand ran a few feet, dropped to the ground and signed it in the blood from his wrist. This time Rosen slammed William to the ground without a thought of the appearance of brutality and sat on him till Bundy brought the bandage.

"You just added assault and resisting arrest to your charges," Rosen said merrily.

"Okay, Barry, tow this to the station. Follow us," Bundy said.

"Whoa, I have a signed release form; this car's going to the FBI crime lab," Mahoney said. William smiled at the defeated look on Rosen's face.

"Yeah, keep smiling. Yer never gonna see the light of day again," Rosen said as he dragged William to the police car.

"Will you let me know if you find something?" William yelled at Mahoney. Mahoney was too far away for his answer to be heard. "What? Speak up," William requested desperately. The reply was still unheard. "Get Timmy! You're my only hope, Mahoney. Is this how it ends? Find him. I was wronged. Don't let the pigs win. Don't let 'em win! He's just a *them* but I'm an *us*."

Rosen paid no attention to William's gibberish. William still couldn't hear Mahoney's response. The car door slammed and they drove away. Still, William continued his babbling while watching the image of Mahoney standing by the Lincoln get farther and farther away and his reality getting closer and closer.

Mahoney was pleased Rosen saved the unpleasantness of having to tell William that he had no choice but to arrest him and turn him in after the car was signed over.

"Well William, you sure fucked this case up," Rosen said.

"It was already fucked up. Timmy got away with it."

"Yes, but now you had to get the feds involved and get yourself arrested."

Rosen, Bundy and Beckworth and a certain-to-be-guilty William were now seated in the interrogation room. .

"So," Beckworth asked. "You broke into Officer Rosen's home and tried to kill an officer of the law."

"Listen, I--"

"Tried to kill Rosen," Bundy abruptly interrupted. "We know."

"He confessed!" Rosen added.

"That does it. I'm not saying shit."

"Good, 'cause there's nothing to say," Rosen stated. "'Cause your charges are breaking and entry, theft of evidence, assault with a deadly weapon against a peace officer, eluding a police vehicle, obstruction of justice for stealing that report and handing it to an unfriendly source, another assault on a peace officer, destruction of private property when you destroyed that yard, and resisting arrest."

Without delay he was fingerprinted and sent to the county jail. The next morning he found himself before Judge Foster. Rosen was there with the district attorney.

"William Defreno, you don't have counsel yet. Do you wish to wait till you do?"

"No, I never got one last time. This is only a first appearance. I tell you right now I waive reading and plead not guilty to all counts."

"Your honor," District Attorney James Reef said, "William Defreno is an extreme danger to the public and a flight risk. We have a report from the guards that he said 'I'll end you,' and was referring to Rosen. We ask no bail."

William knew he made no such comment but it wouldn't matter.

"Granted. William Defreno, you will be held without bail until at least your preliminary hearing. A public defender will be assigned to you and you will return one month from today."

On the way out William got to meet his new public defender. Relief washed over him that it wasn't Don Linbege.

"Hello, I'm Kevin London. I'm your public defender." Although Kevin looked like a lawyer in his blue suit, with slim body, clean face and puffed hair that parted in the middle, it was going to be nearly impossible to win this case. Last time he had the comfort of knowing he was innocent, but now he was guilty and just wanted to get away with it.

The guards escorted William away and informed Kevin he could see his new client at the jail.

On the day of the preliminary a jaded William was dragged to court. After thirty days in jail while Timmy ran free he comprehended of the true meaning of the term "injustice." If it wasn't for the hunt for justice on Timmy and a tight watch at the jail he would've hung himself in his cell.

"Okay William," Kevin said. "Like we discussed in jail this isn't the trial; this is just a hearing to decide whether it goes to trial, like a before-trial. After this we can decide whether we should take an offer from the DA or risk a trial."

As the court was very secure, the arm and leg restraints stayed on for no other visible reason than to torment William more.

"Your honor," Reef said. "I would like to call my first and only witness, Officer Rosen."

Rosen took the stand. Instead of acting the typical timid victim of having been almost killed, Rosen seemed blissful as he looked at chained-up William and took the stand.

"You swear to tell the truth, the whole truth, and nothing but the truth?"

"I do."

"On the night in question could you describe in your own words what happened?"

"Yes, I was at my apartment. I heard a noise and got up to see what it was. I didn't see anything so I let it go. Next thing I knew I was forced down and a man was aiming a gun inches away from my face."

"Do you recognize the person who was aiming the gun at you?"

"Yes. It's the defendant, William Defreno."

"What else happened?"

"He was mad at me."

"Why?"

"In April his girlfriend was killed. I arrested the young man who did it. The young man got off on a technicality, a police mistake."

"Who made that mistake?"

"It was me. I made an illegal search of a trunk. He was enraged that I was the one who made a mistake that let his girlfriend's killer run free. He told me he was going to kill me and I could see he was enraged."

"Had he ever said anything to you concerning your mistake?"

"Yes. In court he told me I should feel bad and that there was no excuse for it."

"Why did he steal your files?"

"I told him I had taken the case files home with me to see if there was anything I could do. At that point he asked where they were and told me since he was going to kill me there would be no need for me to have them. He went to my desk and took them all."

"How were you able to save yourself?"

"I used trickery. I told him that he had me and it wasn't necessary to kill me. The last thing he said before leaving was that if I told anyone he would hunt me down and kill me. That is why I was so persistent on asking no bail. If he gets out I can't sleep at night. The sad part is I have worked very hard to try to undo the mistake and yet William still wants me dead."

"Thank you. Now as for eluding police and destruction of private property do you see that man in the car who was eluding you?"

"It is also William Defreno."

"What happened in your own words?"

"I went to pull over the defendant. I had been to the hotel where he was living and he had snuck out when we arrived. I saw him and attempted to pull him over. We got to about eighty-five. He drove onto a residential lawn and destroyed the grass. My police car got stuck in the mud and he got a head start. I tried to catch up, but unfortunately for me a train was coming and he drove between the barriers and got across. By the time I caught up the train was blocking my access to him."

"Thank you. Now the other assault charge and the resisting arrest; can you tell me in your own words what happened?"

"Yes. I went to the impound yard to look at the defendant's car."

"Why?"

"I hoped to find an address or something that would tell me where he might go. I knew he had lived in California for a while but I didn't have an address. When I went there I saw the defendant trying to pick up his car. I told him to stop and informed him that he was under arrest. He had someone with him who I was not able to identify. The defendant punched me in the chest and escaped. Within a minute I had him back in custody."

"Could you identify the defendant?"

"It is also William Defreno."

"Thank you. No further questions."

Kevin took his turn. The desperation on his face showed. He knew his client was guilty. William felt a little more ready to battle since Rosen's testimony wasn't quite how it had happened. Still he knew it made no difference and he probably would go to jail soon.

"Okay, Officer Rosen, if my client set out to kill you what could you have possibly said that would change his mind?"

"I don't really know. I did a year of hostage negotiation courses and I just know what to say."

"But if he were so deranged, as you say, he would've killed you before you had a chance to stop it."

"Look, I never charged him with attempted murder. I would say William's only intention was to assault me and scare me for an honest mistake I made. I remember telling him that I understood his anger but that this was wrong. Whether or not he was going to kill me makes no difference. He broke into my home, stole evidence and assaulted me."

"Can you understand it? You were the one who set Timothy Hamlin free."

"I didn't set him free. I made a mistake and I feel horrible. What William did was no mistake. It was planned and carried out."

"I'm done," Kevin said, knowing it was going from bad to worse.

"Your honor," Reef said, "I can call two witnesses who saw William at the impound yard."

"No need. I have all I need and I find there is plenty of non circumstantial evidence to prove guilt beyond reasonable doubt and I will proceed with the trial. Both parties shall be ready in sixty days. The defendant shall continue to be held without bail. We're adjourned. Take the defendant back to the lock up."

"Okay," Kevin said. "I'm going to see what kind of plea bargain we can get. I'll see you back at the jail."

William nodded.

The next morning William got up only to see he was still in jail even after a dream that he was out. At breakfast a cheery inmate named Derek wanted to talk. William had always brushed him away, but Derek wanted to be friends with everyone. The young man with a crew cut and one hundred and eighty pounds under his orange jump suit seemed happy and almost like this was where he wanted to be. His sunk-in face and big nose seemed not to bother him at all.

Without ever admitting it out loud this was the best place for Derek. All his friends were here, three meals a day, easy work, free healthcare, no eviction notices, heat and air conditioning, workshop classes and with everything being on a schedule no brain power was needed to survive this simple life. His upbeat attitude only made William angry that everyone else seemed okay with the fact they were in jail and he was the only one who didn't enjoy the atmosphere.

"Hey William, I heard you're going to go to trial."

"Yep."

"You know, corrections is much better than the county jail."

"Really?" William said, just wanting to enjoy his lousy morning coffee with spoiled milk in it.

"Yeah, they got a gym, sports teams, workshops, and you get to move around more. We can smoke and have more visiting hours. This fuckin' place we just sit here all day."

"I take it you've been in corrections?"

"Yeah, did two ta three for a B and E."

"Why are you back?"

"Some bullshit about being in a stolen car."

"Well I guess I'll see you when we get there and you can tell me all about it."

"Oh sure. Come on man, you're the only one who ain't with it. Hey, I got some magazines."

"Naa."

"Hey, come on man, what brand you smoke, the first pack is on me."

"That's all right. I'll see ya at lunch."

"Sure man, no problem, When you're ready to talk we will."

By lunchtime he got to meet Kevin in private.

"Okay, I got an offer from the DA."

"Go on."

"The combined charges could be punished up to ten years or more. I mean if you get convicted you will get a minimum of six and as high as fifteen. The offer is you serve the minimum six and four years suspended."

"Oh my God does that deal suck," William said sarcastically.

"Well, I agree but they have you. There is no disputing it. The jury won't care about the loss of your girlfriend and Rosen and the DA are pushing for the max. In my opinion they'll get it. Come on, you're here without bail. That means they consider you dangerous."

"I know, but I wanna go to trial."

"Oh man, why?"

"I wanna lose in a blaze of glory."

"If that's what you want I'll do what I can. You have to understand something. You aren't going to win because the jury will think you're a hero. I won't let you try to argue that you're in the right. If I defend you and go to trial we argue diminished capacity. Pretty much you're mind was too far gone to comprehend what you did. I want you to go through some therapy and show that you were diminished at the time, but now you feel better."

"I get it. Yeah, when I was free and had a dead girl and a free killer on my hands I was insane. But now that I've spent thirty days in jail and gonna spend another sixty and still have a dead girl and a free Timmy I feel better."

"Look, I know you know a bit about the law. I mean, heck, you defended yourself last time. But you also lost. Yes, justice is a game. Therapy can be very useful and can help this trauma. You must show some sort of recovery, some sort of realization that you didn't know what you were doing because it seems to me you don't fully understand what you did."

"I will do it to save myself. I'll go on and on at the trial about how much better I am and how out of my mind I was. But off the record the only therapy I need is to see Timmy brought to justice."

"I think Rosen was trying to do that, but you messed it up."

"That Rosen is a liar and an ass. He never wanted to help me."

"Well I'm sorry you feel that way. Anyway, I'll visit you a week before trial and we'll go over everything. I'm going to get you enrolled in therapy and I want you to cooperate."

"Fine."

"You'll make it."

"Easy for you to say. Every day in here is like a month. I about lost my mind over thirty days. Now I got sixty more."

Chapter 13

Kangaroo Court

Within ten days William was sitting in his first therapy session. One glance at the therapist was all it took for an embittered William to form a nasty opinion of her. She was probably the same age as him, long brown hair, beautiful face, a twig body and a little wedding ring from someone luckier than himself.

"Hi, I'm Karla," she said as she stuck her tiny soft hand out toward William.

"Hello."

"Well, I've read your case and--" Her cell phone rang. "Hold on."

"Hello, oh hey, honey. Yes I will." She giggled. "No, I didn't. Well I guess we'll just have to go to the Olive Garden till it's fixed." She giggled some more. "No, okay, love ya honey, bye."

Being forced to listen in on a phone conversation between two people who had not a care nor a worry and were just hopelessly in love like he and Annie might've been put a menacing look on his face. He glared directly into her pretty glowing eyes. Without delay the girl requested the guards restrain William.

What a bitch! William thought as he was chained to the chair.

"Okay," she continued in a happy tone. "Tell me about your parents."

"Well I only had one; my dad is gone."

"In prison?"

"No, he died as a result of his service in Vietnam."

"I bet that was quite traumatizing to you seeing your father die."

"Actually I was too young to see it. What was more traumatizing was that everyone else just thinks you're white trash if someone dies of an illness."

"I see. Well today I would like to explore just how much abuse you suffered growing up"

"By the police force here, horrible amounts; I've been falsely arrested over and over, stopped, ticketed for no reason. Now they let the guy who killed Annie walk."

"I mean at home. I feel there is some sort of young traumatic experience that is triggering your behavior."

"Okay, in third grade once the teacher didn't call on me when I had my hand raised."

"William, I don't appreciate the sarcasm. Were your parents full of sarcasm?"

"I don't know what to tell you. This was what caused me to do this. I could'a been a *them* like you are but someone decided to throw a gun in my hand and make me fight. I feel like my dad musta; just drafted in a war I can't win."

"This Rosen guy claimed you were pretty deranged when doing this. He was just trying to help you. He made a mistake and you scared him half to death."

"Half of what he said is untrue and the other half is an exaggeration. Yes, I went in there to get the reports and scare him. But that was crap about how he conned me into letting him live. I didn't wanna kill him. I just wanted to know why he hid the reports."

"There are better ways of asking than breaking into his house and aiming a gun at him."

"I'd like to hear them. I bet if I had just asked he would've denied ever knowing about it. And this crap about how he was trying to get Tim was bull. He's probably happy Tim got away with it. Heck, he helped do it."

"Okay, back to your childhood. How were problems solved in your household?"

"They got solved one way or another."

"Problems didn't get swept away they got solved."

"If something needed to be done it got done. I don't know what you want exactly."

"I see. No matter what it took things stayed in order?"

"I guess."

"You came from a home that aggressively took care of problems and unsolved business. Is that fair to say?"

"Yeah, sure." William replied watching her assertively take notes on everything he said.

"Was there a place you liked to go when you were a kid? Let's say around ten years old."

"I guess the Circle K; it had Slurpees and pinball machines, it was fun to hang out at."

"You went there and felt safe and a good place to get away from home?"

"I guess."

"Kind of a home away from home?"

"I liked it, they had an arcade and cheap candy, yeah it was sometimes my home away from home."

"Did you think about the Circle K even when you weren't there?"

"Yeah."

"Maybe even dream you were there even when you were at home or school? Or even pretend being there when things were not fun at home or school?"

"Oh yeah, I really miss the days when something as simple

as a Circle K could bring so much joy. I daydreamed about it a lot and sometimes I still do. I was a kid with not a care or worry looking forward all day to going and drinking sugar and playing pinball. Before the Casners, the girls, the police and before everything went to hell."

Not wanting to miss out on her court fees and having the ambition to show her supervisor she was doing a good job she attended the evidentiary hearing ready to testify for William.

"It is my professional opinion that William had horrible events happen to him as a kid. Very traumatic abuse from home. An abused kid will run away to a safe place. Often William ran away to a local Circle K where he felt safe from home. He mentioned this place was like a home away from home.

"As a result, when a child is abused he can block out what is going on and become something like an object or there is something that separates him from the world. William would pretend he was at this Circle K when things got too heated at home. An abused child can do more than daydream about something they can physically remove their mind from the current dwelling and be in that place. This ability stays with him as an adult. William admitted he still goes to his safe Circle K.

"In William's case I feel he was so angry about the mistake Rosen made that he felt like he was being abused. Like an abused child he, as an adult, blocked out his actions. His physical body may have entered Rosen's apartment but his mind was blank. He was something or someone else."

"What makes you think that for sure, doctor?" Kevin asked.

"I looked at the transcripts of Rosen's testimony. William insisted that this was not accurate. This tells me he doesn't remember what happened because his mind wasn't really there. It seems he was hazy about what happened and never gave a true motive for doing it."

"But why would he do this even on an unconscious level?"

"Well, William came from a household that aggressively took care of problems. If something was wrong it would be corrected even if it meant someone got hurt. If William did anything that was a problem it was taken care of aggressively. No breaks, no mercy. Coming from this and the trauma from his past, his mind might of gone into a kind of autopilot.

"He was brainwashed as a child that he must solve any wrongdoing and thinking. This Rosen wronged him in his mind; and in his mind he solved it without really comprehending what he did.

"Afterward, his eluding police and resisting arrest only confirms his capacity. I mean why else would he fight three cops with guns at the impound yard? He didn't stand a chance of getting away from them but his delusions made him believe he would."

"Okay, doctor, is it your testimony that William Defreno was at a diminished capacity during the time he committed these acts?"

"Yes."

"Thank you." Kevin sat down. Reef took his turn. William just sat nauseated at her lack of understanding and total drive to believe just what she wanted and further her career.

"If you give this testimony at trial how can you explain that he didn't know what he was doing?"

"Like I said, as a child--"

"Yeah, yeah, he pretended he was a balloon when he was abused."

"I don't think you understand. He wouldn't pretend to be an object. His mind would literally shut off and he would become someone else. It's hard to explain, but at trial I will show in great detail what I mean."

"How much will you be paid to give this testimony?"

"Roughly fifteen hundred plus expenses."

"Expenses like what? A massage and a spa treatment?"

"Mr. Reef," Foster said, "just continue."

Even though Reef was the enemy William wanted to give him a good handshake for that wisecrack.

"Well, let's say you're right. If released, how can we be sure he won't go on autopilot again and do something else he won't remember?"

"This can be treated. I have ordered him to take anti-psychotic medications.

By next week he'll be on a neurotransmitter called Dopamine. This is thought to be relevant to schizophrenia. Before trial I would like to try Amisulpride, Clozapine and maybe some Lithium. These will aid in ending his delusional thinking and can relieve episodes of psychotic behavior. With treatment, a person such as Mr. Defreno can make a full recovery and not be a threat to society."

"Are you going to give him this treatment?"

"I have been treating him and have seen great improvement even without the meds."

"In just thirty days? If he is released will you continue to treat him? How will we know he's taking his meds?"

"I could."

"You could? You're a jailhouse psychiatrist and therapist."

"I work with the general public as well."

"Yes, but your main focus is on prisoners. The only way William could continue to get help from you is to stay in jail."

"I could pass this on to another therapist just as capable as me."

"How can we be sure William will go to treatment if released?"

"That's not up to me. All I can say is in most cases once a person is on the meds he sees the error in his thinking and voluntarily continues to use them without a court order."

"But it might be better just to keep him in jail to make sure?"

"It would be pointless to incarcerate him. It would be the same as keeping a person who had the flu away from everyone once they've recovered. William is the same. He just has a strong flu. Only in this case it's a mental flu. Once the meds and therapy kick in he will be fine."

"How long does this take?"

"About six weeks altogether. I've been working on him for thirty days and once he starts the meds by trial my opinion is he will be a normal person and pose no threat to himself or others. Realistically, once the meds kick in he would probably pass a lie detector saying he didn't do this. And, really he didn't, once an abused mind becomes chemically imbalanced it can cause behavior problems beyond ones control; his mind is just in need of help."

"Your honor, if they want to put this expert on to say William is diminished I won't object. This only proves how dangerous William Defreno is."

"Okay, the witness will be admitted to testify at trial. You may step down."

"Also, your honor, I would ask that Mr. Defreno's prior arrest be admitted."

"I object, your honor. He--"

"Save it. Mr. Defreno was acquitted of those charges and they were sealed. I won't allow them to be used. Also I don't think the jury hearing the story of how Mr. Hamlin's parents paid off law enforcement to make that arrest will help anything."

"Okay. I feel confident with what we have," Reef said.

"Adjourned."

A steaming and embarrassed William was escorted back to jail. He would have to see Karla many more times before trial. He could only ponder the great effects his new medication would have on him.

That night he pondered how others have served years in prison. He'd only been here forty five days and the effects were atrocious. He knew he was affected much more harshly than others, even to the point of feeling like an *us*. He wondered how crazy his mind would get before it perished.

In the next therapy session Karla didn't have William chained. She flipped open her little notebook and got comfortable in her chair even though wearing a business skirt made it tricky. For a split second William got a quick peak and was let down to see she *was* wearing panties.

"How are you holding up?" She asked with an uninformed idea of what was going on.

"I've become an element of my cell; no longer a visitor, but simply a furnishing or fixture dwelling dumbly within the concrete rubric cube of hell from which there is no escape."

"So," she replied slowly, dismissing what she just heard. "What changes have you noticed since you've started the meds? Any new ideas about what you did at Rosen's house and the effects you had on him?"

"I think it's just making me ignore what a need to do. I have deep concerns."

"What concerns do you have?"

"The constant frog in my throat concerns me, but I know better than to request medical attention here."

"What have you observed as far as the reality of what you've done and what could happen to you?"

"I see why everyone wants to be a *them*."

"What?"

Without delay William, who was becoming the nutcase she had painted him to be, once again presented his *us* and *them* speech. Being a *them,* Karla just smiled and decided to order higher milligrams of the medication for him. William's rage kicked up at the reality that she was living a little fairy tale life and seemed to enjoy rubbing it in his face in a settle kind of way.

"William, it's very likely you may go to prison. What are your thoughts on how you will deal with that?"

"I was the man on the grassy knoll," William mumbled.

"What was that? I didn't hear you," she replied thinking there was no way he just said what she thought he just said.

"I said, um, ah, I know 'the man' can be a real asshole." Karla frowned at William's use of cursing, but was glad it wasn't what she thought.

"My friend Derek has spoken to me about how to get through prison time. Heck, he looks like he's looking forward to it, so I guess all I can do is hope I can make it as well. But I have most of my energy focused on winning."

"Yes, but if I can't successfully get you into a treatment center instead of prison you must be prepared for it. It will be hard and I know corrections isn't as concerned with keeping you on the proper medication. That's why you must open up more to me, I need to know the extent of your abusive childhood. I will give you this next week and I want you to write down the earliest event you can remember of something bad happening. I want a full page and maybe some artwork to go with it."

William realized just how bad it was; her idea of winning was getting him into the nut house while his idea was to walk.

"It's just a reality I must face. I realize it's most likely I'm going to the big house. I never heard from the FBI so I assume Timmy won't be joining me."

"I'm glad to see you are not delusional about it. It will be hard, but it's not like on TV. You can have an active life and be safe. But, you must have a stable mind and be in touch with reality. This may be your only change to get help.

"In prison you could actually better yourself. Many women want to pen-pal with male prisoners. You could get a full college education. Maybe meet a new friend or two. I want you to also this week make a list of the positive things that could come out of you being incarcerated."

"Okay."

"Alright, keep taking yer meds and I'm going to lower the Amisulpride dosage because I feel you're much calmer than you were when we started. I will increase the Dopamine for now and when I see more improvement I'll lower it."

William smiled for the first time in months. Karla took it as the counseling and meds bringing his mind back to normal. She didn't need to know the real reason was all this time he was and would continue to fake taking the pills to please Karla.

On the big day William was brought to the courthouse. The judge, jury, DA and his public defender were all in place. It wouldn't be more than a one-day trial since Rosen and Karla were the only witnesses. William had already made up his mind that this was it. Ninety days in jail had dragged on forever. It was no secret that it was just a drop in the bucket compared to the amount of time he'd have by the end of the day.

Life was over for him. Any joy and any will to survive was gone. He didn't even plan to give his best efforts and had no hope in the trial. His mind was completely corrupted and even the memory of he and Annie so happy together didn't seem real. It seemed more like a movie he had watched than a real part of his life.

"Your honor, I wish to call Officer Rosen to the stand,"

Reef said.

William rolled his eyes at the thought of Rosen telling again of the horrors that had been committed upon him. After a few moments William wondered where Rosen was.

Chapter 14

A Few Guilty Men

"Is Rosen in the restroom?" Foster asked.

"I don't know," Reef replied.

"Sorry, your honor," a court officer said. "We have Rosen here; we just got stuck in traffic."

The jury, judge and William became suddenly bewildered and befuddled. The guards were carrying Rosen into the room in chains.

"What the hell is going on?" Foster demanded.

"He was supposed to be in court today and here he is. I don't really know what you mean," the guard replied.

"I want to know what the hell is going on, now!"

"Perhaps I can explain," a nicely dressed man said as he approached the bench.

"Who are you?"

"Agent Mahoney, FBI."

"This is a state court, not federal."

"Yes, but I can explain everything."

"Well, you seem to be the only one."

"Officer Rosen, or shall I say just Mr. Rosen, is in federal custody."

"Why?"

"Well, I guess word doesn't get around too much. Mr. Rosen accepted a plea agreement with one of your DA's that would clear him of all state charges if he pled guilty to the federal crime of conspiracy to kidnapping resulting in death."

"You better start talking faster because he is the key

witness in our case."

"I know, but the court should know the story."

"Go ahead."

"After finding a piece of evidence in the truck of William Defreno's car we determined the murder victim, Jennifer Annie Lewis, was alive when Mr. Hamlin knowingly kidnapped her when she was in need of urgent care. He had no intention of driving her to any hospital and when she did get to the hospital she was DOA. From her injuries she may've survived if she was treated faster.

"Mr. Defreno was trying to get her to a hospital for that fast treatment. Mr. Hamlin stole his car knowing to the full extent of her medical need and didn't help her. Which means she died as a result of the kidnapping. Under the Federal Statues the illegal search Rosen did may not've applied at the time to the Federal Crime Mr. Hamlin committed. The State suppressed the body and weapon, but her being kidnapped can still be charged without the body or weapon. "

"What does this have to do with Rosen?"

"Well, Timothy Hamlin was arrested last month for this. We were seeking life with no parole. Rather than challenge the charge, Mr. Hamlin's attorney informed us he had a very tasty, as he put it, story to tell. We had to offer him a deal, but it was worth it. Mr. Hamlin cannot now receive more than twenty years, but told us how he and Mr. Rosen planned it.

"Basically Mr. Hamlin had money from his parents. They had stashed a great deal of cash in a deposit box under a different name. After Mr. Defreno's testimony put Randy and Carol Casner away, Mr. Rosen and Mr. Hamlin came up with a plan. For a hundred grand, Mr. Rosen would pull him over that day and intentionally mess up the search to secure Mr. Hamlin's freedom.

"They actually had two-way radios and Rosen made sure

no other cops were in the area when it happened. Mr. Hamlin pretended to be in poverty along with Mr. Rosen. In five years Mr. Rosen was going to retire early and take the money and run. He even intentionally removed the reports to make sure the case was never reopened or investigated.

"It was actually William Defreno's criminal act that got the case to the FBI."

"Oh my goodness."

"But Mr. Rosen is ready to testify in this case."

Mahoney's smugness indicated that by law Rosen still needed to testify. The look on the jury members' and the judge's faces confirmed that this case had been misrepresented.

"William Defreno, as the judge I can't just drop the charges. You still committed the crimes whether or not the means justified the end, and you can't break the law."

"Your honor," Kevin interrupted.

"Save it, counsel. Anyway we will need to find a new jury if you wish to continue. Here is my offer. All arrest charges expunged, ninety days in jail and twenty hours community service. Since you've already served the ninety days you can walk out of here today with no criminal record after your twenty hours is complete."

Without asking Kevin's permission William stood up.

"I accept. Please get these chains off me."

"Deal is accepted by the defendant. You will have six months to complete your services. I will recommend that you spend those twenty hours re-sodding the lawn you destroyed to avoid civil charges. Mr. Rosen's testimony will not be necessary and the jury is dismissed with the thanks of the court."

All Rosen saw of William was a defiant stare as they took the chains off him.

"Wow, I never thought we'd win this one," Kevin said.

"I know."

"What are you going to do now William?"

"Well, Kevin, I think tonight I'll go home and sleep. Hold on," William said as he went to get Agent Mahoney who was walking by.

"Agent Mahoney, what did you find in that trunk?"

"Well, Tim's sentencing is next Thursday at the Federal courthouse. Be there at ten sharp."

"But what was it?"

"Well, ethically, I can't tell you till he's sentenced. Even then I probably shouldn't. But after he's sentenced come by the office and I'll show you what we found."

Chapter 15

Washing Away

On the sentencing day for Timothy Hamlin William showed up in his new suit. Instead of wearing his usual miserable expression he could actually feel a little normal today. As Timmy was brought out in his orange jumpsuit before the judge, William actually smiled.

"Your honor," Mahoney said, "I wanted Tim to give a statement as part of our deal."

"What kind of statement?"

"Just me asking the contents of his plan and him admitting the true intentions of the plan."

"Sure." Mahoney looked at William in the audience and smiled.

"Mr. Hamlin, who was the intended target on the day of the murder?"

"It was William's girl. I figured it would be worse to kill her than him."

"That is all."

"Mr. Hamlin," Federal Judge Nero said, "I have reviewed everything with this case. I would normally impose life with no parole or even death. Your cooperation was very helpful in arresting Officer Rosen. This was an effort that couldn't have succeeded without your help. You are also lucky that no state charges will be brought against you.

"I found this to be a planned and premeditated act with little or no remorse shown. I will give you some leniency as promised by the DA. However not much. I hereby sentence you to ten to twenty years in the Federal penitentiary. We're adjourned."

"Well, Annie, I did it," William said to himself. The last glimpse of Timmy was burned into his mind as they heaved him away. All the trouble through the years was being hauled away. His mind entered a deeper mode as he thought of where he would be if not for Timmy and his family. The guilt that the bullet had been meant for him was no more.

"I don't know, I'd probably be, I don't know, probably not here," he said to himself. A man and woman approached William. He knew he'd seen them before but had been too preoccupied the last couple of months to remember.

"Hello William," she said.

"Oh my!" William said as he remembered by sound of her voice that she was Annie's mother, Sara. The two sounded so much alike that for just a split second he thought it was Annie.

"What are you guys doing here?"

"We came to see Timmy get sentenced."

"Well, I wish it could've been more."

"He won't last more than a month," Annie's dad, Robert said.

"I'm sorry I didn't go to the funeral, but I sent you guys all the money."

"We didn't care about the money," Sara said with a smile.

"Well, I thought it was the least I could do."

"You made her very happy, William, Don't blame yourself for what happened."

"I wish I didn't."

"Hey," Robert interrupted. "You got Timmy. You were the only one who stood up for Annie. I mean I heard you almost went to jail yourself for twenty years to get evidence to put Tim away."

"Yeah, I guess you're right. I just have passion for what I

do. I guess I really am an *us*."

"What?"

"Never mind. Anyway, I'm glad you guys came to see me."

"Yeah," Sara said. "Come back to see us sometime, okay?"

"I will," William replied as the three moved toward the door to depart.

Agent Mahoney approached William just as he was about to open the doors of the courtroom. He still hadn't got over the bombshell of the parents when Mahoney said, "Hello. I got your paperwork ready for you to get your car back."

"I don't think I want it."

"Well, I'm sure you want me to show you what we found."

"Of course, but then burn the car."

"Oh that's nonsense."

William got in Mahoney's car and they drove to the crime lab where the car was being stored. For the second time, the first being to the impound yard, the ride in a law enforcement vehicle was pleasant.

"Look, William, I know this might be hard, but I'll waive the impound fees you owe us and I'll have it scrubbed from top to bottom. Just please pick it up tomorrow after we look at it."

"Oh, okay, I mean I did have the car before Annie and I guess I can drive it after her."

"Good. I'm glad to see that jail therapist helped you."

"They didn't help me, you did. You could've just brushed me off as a paranoid freak or just said you're too busy to do this. Nobody else ever listened. Lawyers don't care unless you are willing to plop down money. The police didn't care and in fact harbored Rosen and Marshall. The counselors just wanted me to say my parents horribly abused me and that I was temporarily insane.

"Nobody else ever helped, but you did. You listened even though it sounded so absurd. You went out on the line and got it done. I thank you more than anyone else. You are truly an *us*."

"A what?"

"Forget it. Just know that it means you are different from the rest."

"Well, it is my job. I remember the anonymous letter you sent last year about the Casners. Yes, I thought it was just a prank. In fact I've dealt with thousands of pranks and false alarms. It's like a fire alarm; most are accidents or pranks, but the fire department responds ready to go every time just because the one time it's real they're ready. It was times like yours that showed me it was worth hearing all the false stories to finally get a real case. I thank you."

They arrived and walked toward the Lincoln parked behind the gates.

"So what's that medication like?"

"I don't know. I sold it to my jailhouse friend Derek for Cokes."

Mahoney just smiled and pretended he hadn't heard that.

"Ya know, it's been eating at me; what did you find that proved Annie was still alive when she was in the trunk? I mean enough so that Timmy spilled his guts."

"Well," Mahoney replied as he opened the trunk and handed William a small flashlight. "You'll have to crawl in there and find out. It's on the top right corner."

William crawled inside. The sight of dried blood was disturbing, but not as much as before. He shone the light all around but didn't see anything.

"Hey, Mahoney, what am I looking for?"

"You'll know when you see it. Just look in the top right."

William looked as he was told and knew in an instant what he had found. His heart sank as he saw the words, "bye wi" written in dried blood on the top of the metal frame of the trunk. The "wi" was smeared as in indication she wanted to write "William" but got too weak or something blocked her. William got back out and faced Mahoney.

"We needed to get this to a crime lab to determine for sure that it was her blood and that her finger wrote it. Sure enough it was and this proved she was alive when Tim stole your car."

"Well, I guess he's got ten to twenty years to think about it now."

"Yep, but I hope you don't think about it that long."

"Nope, I won't. I'll take the car after you wash it good."

"Good, because it's a pain to sell these after they've been used in a crime."

"It'll be kinda creepy, but I think Annie would want me to just use it."

"Good. Come by tomorrow."

"Thank you," William said followed by a handshake.

The next week William spent his time putting new sod in at the house with the lawn he had destroyed. With only about four sections to go his community service was nearly complete. A car pulled up to the house just as he unloaded another roll of sod. At first he didn't pay much attention because he knew the owners of the house were inside.

The young girl who came out of the car struck him as familiar. Then he remembered her name was Andrea and he had had a crush on her in high school, but she had hated him.

"Oh, not done yet?" Andrea said.

"What brings you here?"

"My parents live here. I did too till I went to college."

"Oh, what are the odds I'd pick your house to destroy?"

"I don't know. I thought you were dead but I guess you wanted to swing by and say hello. Make sure you put that grass side up."

"Yeah, well actually I'm almost done. What is your

major?"

"Psychology. I hope to be a counselor one day."

"Fun, next time I get in trouble you can tell 'em how I turn into a balloon when I'm abused."

"Or turn into a jackass whenever yer around a girl."

"Or turn to jelly when I see you."

"Yeah, anyway what about you? Are you going to college?"

"I don't know. Every time I think about school this town tries to get me thrown in the hole for twenty years."

"Well, you always manage to dodge the bullet."

"I guess, but ya know it seems another one's just around the corner."

"You should get a degree in Criminal Justice."

"Yeah, that would be quite fun. Yer parents don't seem too mad. They actually understood."

"Well, I'll be inside when you're done. We could have a cold drink and you can tell me all about it."

"Okay, sure." William said, wondering why the offer. In his mind he assumed she hated him and he might still be right, but at least he'd be given the opportunity to find out.

Did you enjoy this book?

Send questions or comments to the author:

Dave Aquino
PO Box 741351
Arvada, CO. 80006

Check out other books by this author:

Personal War

Counselor

The Slot Machine

www.ingramcontent.com/pod-product-compliance
Lightning Source LLC
Chambersburg PA
CBHW052142170626
46812CB00004B/1557

9780980919110